FATHER OF
CONVENIENCE

Other books by Katrina Thomas:

Everything Wright

FATHER OF CONVENIENCE

•

Katrina Thomas

AVALON BOOKS
NEW YORK

Published by Thomas Bouregy & Co., Inc.
160 Madison Avenue, New York, NY 10016

Library of Congress Cataloging-in-Publication Data

Thomas, Katrina, 1959–
Father of convenience / Katrina Thomas.
        p. cm.
ISBN 978-0-8034-9913-3 (acid-free paper)
1. Journalists—Fiction.   2. Birthfathers—Fiction
3. Single mothers—Fiction.   4. Domestic
fiction.   I. Title.

PS3620.H629F38 2008
813'.6—dc22

                        2008017328

PRINTED IN THE UNITED STATES OF AMERICA
ON ACID-FREE PAPER
BY HADDON CRAFTSMEN, BLOOMSBURG, PENNSYLVANIA

For Kent, who went to Saudi Arabia,
for Jeff, who went to the Red Sea,
for Brian, who went to Iraq,
and for their families who stayed at home
worrying about and hoping for their safe return.

Chapter One

Baghdad, Iraq

"We're moving out!"

Andres Nunez tapped out the last paragraph of the article he was writing on his notebook computer as shouts echoed through the hall outside the open door of his hotel room. He did not look up as his friend and colleague, Karl Simpson, pulled trousers and shirts from the closet they shared and stuffed the items into a canvas duffel bag.

"The east side of the building is gone, Andres. There are other bombs. You don't have time to finish."

Andres struck a key to save the document and then slipped a flash drive into one of the USB ports on the side of the computer. "I need just a few more seconds to make a backup copy."

"We have transportation to Kuwait City. I'm not going to die here, and I won't let you stay to die either." Karl zipped the duffel bag and slung the strap over one shoulder. "Get your things and let's go!"

Andres slid the flash drive into the left pocket of his loose-fitting shirt and closed the computer. Single shots of gunfire ripped through the air outside the second-story window as he rose from the chair by the battered wooden desk at which he had been working. He put the computer inside his own canvas bag.

"What are you waiting for?"

Andres did not ignore the fear and impatience evident in his friend's voice as it resounded in his ears, but he took time to glance around the room. "My Saint Isidore medal. It's here somewhere."

"The car won't wait, Andy. The driver will leave without us. We've got to go now."

With a triumphant shout, Andres lifted a sterling silver chain and round medallion from the floor near one leg of a bedside table and slipped it over his head. Taking his bag in one hand, he grasped the wooden cane next to the door and followed Karl out into the deserted hallway.

A stab of pain shot through his left thigh as he rushed down a narrow flight of stairs and tried to keep up with his companion. Stale, hot, stifling air stuck in his nostrils and made breathing difficult. Beads of sweat trickled down the center of his back.

When they reached the ground floor and stepped into the searing afternoon sunlight, a series of sharp sniper shots exploded around the nearby corner of the hotel. Andres resisted the urge to return to the shelter of the building with the intention of writing a firsthand narrative describing the scene of violence and devastation unfolding around him. He knew his editor would definitely appreciate such an account, but, at the last moment, he changed his mind.

Using the cane for support, he hurried behind Karl as his colleague approached the car parked a few feet from them. The driver did not wait for them to close the back doors before he pulled away from the hotel and accelerated along the narrow street toward a route out of the Iraqi capital.

Andres set his duffel bag beside him and rested his head against the back of the lumpy, worn seat. He breathed through the spasms of pain shooting up and down his left leg.

"Honestly, Andres." His companion shook his head. "You take the most reckless chances. I don't know how you can put your life into the hand of the patron saint of farmers when we've received reports that radical Sunni clerics are organizing attacks in this part of Baghdad."

Karl stared at the medal around Andres' neck. "I think you've been pressing your luck with poor Saint Isidore. We both could have been killed back there in that hotel. It's been a possible target of those militant insurgents for over a week now."

Chuckling, Andres clasped the small round medal in his tanned fist. "No challenge is too great for Saint Isidore. My ancestors asked for his protection when they left Spain to start a new life in Argentina over a century ago. Then my great-grandparents took that same devotion to the Spanish saint of farmers when they moved to New Mexico and struggled to turn a piece of undeveloped land into a successful ranch."

Karl sighed. "You're not on a farm now."

"No, but my grandmother gave me this medal the day I told her about my first overseas assignment as a news correspondent. She said that with it, Saint Isidore would always protect me."

"So you think you have some kind of special safe-guard against terrorist attacks and rebel uprisings? Sometimes I think you believe you're invincible."

Andres' thoughts drifted to his southwestern child-hood home for a few moments as the face of a young, grinning, dark-haired boy riding a chestnut stallion crossed his mind. He dropped the medal onto his chest. "No, I just refuse to be afraid to take a few risks."

"A few? With you, Andres, it's a daily occurrence. You never pass up an opportunity to infiltrate an insurgent's hideout or interview a known assassin or track a suspected terrorist. You're thirty-two years old. I would like to think that you'd at least consider the fate of your child if you end up dead. I certainly hope your life insurance premiums are paid."

Andres lifted his brows. "My child? What are you

talking about? You didn't hit your head back there at the hotel, did you?"

"I'm serious. When my son was born, I stopped volunteering for those dangerous assignments. For months now, I've been trying to get a permanent position back home."

"I understand completely, Karl. Jeanne and Timmy need you."

"So what about you?"

"What about me? I have no close family. My parents and grandparents have all died. My wife divorced me and then died in a car crash. I have no reason not to take chances if I want to. In fact, I'm still waiting to be assigned to the West Bank."

He waved a hand toward his left thigh. "I wish this stupid leg would hurry up and heal."

"As if Baghdad isn't dangerous enough. You really want to put yourself in the middle of the fighting between the Israelis and Palestinians at this time in your life?"

Andres watched a shadow cross his friend's face. "You know I've wanted that assignment for years. Why all this fuss now?"

"I'm worried about your lack of commitment to your child."

Andres stared at Karl. "What are you talking about?"

His colleague gave him a puzzled look. "Cheryl had a baby a few months before her automobile accident. My wife saw the child. She told me the baby looks just like you."

"Your wife did what?"

"She ran into Cheryl in a restaurant in Arlington one day."

"My ex-wife had a child?"

"Andres, I just assumed —"

"A baby?"

Karl cleared his throat. "Look, I'm sorry you're finding out this way. I always thought you knew about the child. I guess I thought you were upset about the whole situation, the divorce, the accident, and your own injuries. When you were captured just days before you were supposed to return to Washington for Cheryl's funeral, I realized that the combination of events was a lot for you to face. I thought you were uncomfortable talking about the responsibility of parenthood right then."

His friend's words hit Andres as if he had been thrown from a building during the explosion of a bomb. The muscles in his shoulders tightened as he clenched his jaw.

With his mind racing, he made mental calculations to figure out if such an incredible reality were possible. The last time he had seen Cheryl was two and a half years ago when they had met in Frankfurt for Christmas. He had believed they were getting together for a romantic weekend, but she had stunned him by giving him the ultimatum of quitting his job as a foreign correspondent or ending their marriage. Cheryl insisted she had grown tired of the absences, the uncertainties, and the dangers of his lifestyle.

Andres could not, of course, blame Cheryl. It was unfair to ask one's spouse to live such a life. He never should have married her. They had so little in common. She had grown up wealthy and pampered in New York City. He came from a long line of farmers in the Southwest.

He pulled his thoughts back to Karl and the announcement that he had a child. Cheryl must have been pregnant when they had said good-bye in Frankfurt. Had she known? If she had, she should have told him. He had a right to know that she was carrying his child even if she no longer wanted to be his wife.

The car hit a pothole, and Andres held his breath waiting for the explosion of a land mine, but the driver pushed on without even slowing down. They left the city of Baghdad behind them and followed a road along the Euphrates River.

Andres studied it, the brown ribbon of water and its banks, the site of the birthplace of civilization. After pondering ancient history and the state of the modern world for a few moments, he turned back to Karl. "You're telling me I have a two-year-old child?"

"About two, yes. The child's name is Andy, I believe."

Andres leaned over the front seat and addressed the driver. "How long before we reach Kuwait City, Farid?"

"Eight to nine hours, sir, as long as we have no trouble."

Nodding, Andres sat back against the seat and sighed. Eight hours along dusty, dangerous roads under a sizzling, hot sun and then in the dark, inhospitable night. Eight hours before he could start making calls to get information about his child. In such a short time, his whole world had changed. He had a child. He was a father.

"I have the right to meet Andy, Mrs. Bennett. I'll be there tomorrow."

The man's words on the other end of the telephone had not been demanding or threatening, but they had held a note of urgency that Eve could not ignore. Andres Nunez wanted to see his child.

Hours after he had called, his words were still echoing through her mind. Every time she recalled the sound of his deep voice edged with a mild and appealing Latin accent, her stomach tightened, and her mouth dried.

Andres Nunez. Was it possible that he was alive? After nearly two years thinking he was dead, how could she allow her mind to believe such a shocking turn of events?

She moved around the living room of the waterfront cottage picking up toys, straightening piles of magazines and books, and fluffing sofa pillows as she wondered what was happening. The man could have been lying, of course. He could be an impostor. Andres Nunez could not be alive, could he?

Eve had never met him and had never heard him speak. The man who had called earlier that evening could have been anyone. On the other hand, she could think of no reason why anyone would be lying about being Andy's father.

She sighed. She did not need this complication in her life. Andy's adoption was almost finalized. Why was the child's father suddenly appearing?

She checked on Andy snuggled under a layer of blankets in the lower bunk with only a dark curly head sticking out from beneath the covers. Then she looked in on Tanner in the adjacent room. The little boy had fallen asleep surrounded by his collection of plastic action figures on top of the covers of his full-size bed.

Eve gathered the treasured toys and placed them in a wooden crate she had painted and stenciled with anchors and sailing ships. She pulled the sheet from under the sleeping seven-year-old and covered him before turning off the small ceramic lighthouse lamp on the oak stand that matched his bed frame.

Assured that her children were asleep, she headed for her own bedroom across the hall. Undressing, she stepped into the shower and allowed the cool spray of water to wash over her skin that was still warm and sticky from the typical early July evening on Hatteras Island.

After spending most of the day at the beach, Eve's whole body was sandy and windblown and covered with leftover sunscreen lotion. She scrubbed and lathered until every part of her tingled.

Cleansed and refreshed, she stepped from the shower stall. Wrapping her wavy, shoulder-length hair in a towel, she began to dry herself with another one. She stopped when she heard a noise. She rushed to open her bedroom door to listen. Was one of the children awake?

The sound she heard was not the cry or movement of a child. It was a knock. After a moment, she determined that what she heard was an insistent rapping on the front door.

Pulling her calf-length terry cloth robe on and tying the belt around her waist, she glanced at the alarm clock next to her bed. Ten thirty. Who would be visiting at such an hour?

She hurried through the hall leading to the kitchen and switched on the porch light before swinging open the wooden door. Through the screen of the outer door, she saw a tall, broad-shouldered man in jeans and short-sleeved shirt standing on the porch.

"Mrs. Bennett?"

His voice was quiet with a light Latin accent, the same one she had heard on the telephone earlier that day. In the porch light, his tanned skin looked bronze as he held an identification card with a photograph against the screen of the door.

A strand of thick, dark hair fell across his forehead above high, chiseled cheekbones, and he combed it back with the fingers of one hand as Eve glanced from the picture identification to the man standing on the porch. *Andres Nunez.* His name was printed on the card, and the photograph matched his face.

Eve swallowed as uneasiness mixed with a sense of wonder that made her heart begin to race. So, here he was. Andy's father. Andres Nunez. He had suddenly appeared after all this time.

There was absolutely no doubt about *that* fact as she stared into the large, dark brown eyes. Andy shared the man's thick, dark hair, determined jaw, and narrow face. The child was definitely this man's image; but, still, Andres Nunez was a stranger.

"Mr. Nunez. I didn't expect you until tomorrow."

He shifted his weight and reached for the nearby railing as his mouth tightened into a thin line. He could have been controlling his annoyance, but Eve thought his expression was more like a repressed grimace of pain than one of anger or irritation.

"I called you from Washington this afternoon. I was able to reschedule some appointments, and I drove down as soon as I could. I'm here to see Andy."

She pushed the towel wrapped in a loose turban style back from her forehead, and strands of damp hair fell along both sides of her face. "I'm afraid Andy is asleep, Mr. Nunez, and has been for quite a while."

Bleak, dark eyes stared back at her. "I've come all this way. I won't stay long."

His heartfelt plea threatened to dissolve her cautious determination. Eve's fingers played with the rolled collar of her robe as she considered his request.

"No, Mr. Nunez. Two-year-old children are very cranky when they don't get enough sleep. Come back tomorrow, and you can meet Andy then."

He slipped his identification card in a pocket and

then rubbed the knuckles of one hand along his jawline as though he were thinking about her refusal to allow him to stay. Was he the kind of man who was accustomed to getting his own way all of the time?

If the tall, dark stranger was Andy's father, and Eve had little doubt that he was, his presence now in Andy's life would affect not only the two-year-old but her son, Tanner, as well. The prospect of sharing Andy with Andres Nunez frightened her. Andy was her child and had been for almost two years. She did not want to consider what impact Andres Nunez's arrival would have on her little family.

"It's late, Mr. Nunez. Go get a hotel room in the village and come back tomorrow about ten."

His mouth tightened again, and she thought he would protest; but finally he nodded. The renegade lock of hair swung to the center on his forehead once more. It gave him a boyish, almost mischievous look. "Very well then. Tomorrow, at ten."

Eve's heart pounded as he combed the strand back from his face and gave her a good-bye nod. She could not help but feel empathy for the man who wanted to meet Andy, but she refused to give all of her sympathy to a father who had never, to her knowledge, made a single attempt to contact her or the child before that moment.

Why was Andres Nunez making a personal, and rather insistent, appearance after all of this time? Did he really just want to meet his child, or did he have another purpose in mind? What was he doing? These questions plagued her as she dressed for bed and lay for hours waiting for sleep to come. The image of dark eyes on a narrow bronze face and an unruly lock of dark hair entered her thoughts again and again until the picture of Andres Nunez was a permanent fixture etched in her mind.

"Why can't I ride one of the horses, Mom? I really want to try. Please, Mom."

Eve drove her sport utility vehicle along the tree-lined street of waterfront homes that edged the eastern shore of Pamlico Sound. Pink, white, and yellow blossoms adorned flowering bushes and created a tropical kind of atmosphere in the quiet Hatteras Island neighborhood of North Carolina.

"No horses, Tanner. We're going to take a nice leisurely walk through Buxton Woods. Riding a horse is dangerous. I've never ridden one either."

"But I want to try, Mom. I'm almost eight, you know."

Eve hid a smile as she made a right turn into the sand-packed driveway of small, crushed stones and tiny pieces of broken shells. How many times had she had this same horse riding argument with her son?

"Go in the house and change your clothes, and we'll—"

Her voice trailed off as her eyes caught sight of a small red sports car parked in front of the house. Her stomach somersaulted as her gaze darted to the man with long legs sitting on the third step of the staircase leading to the wood-framed structure supported by thick wooden pylons one story above the ground.

Andres Nunez. His knees nearly touched his tanned chin covered with a shadow of dark beard as he lifted his head to look in her direction. He had wasted no time. It was not even nine thirty yet.

As she brought her car to a stop and turned off the ignition, she saw him push the rebel strand of hair off his forehead. Her pulse jumped before she inhaled a deep, steady breath of air.

"Hey, Mom. Look. Someone's here."

Eve did not have a chance to explain before Tanner unfastened the restraints of his booster seat and scrambled from the vehicle. The little boy bounded across the grass to the tall, dark stranger who rose to his feet and smiled at her young son.

Her hands shook as she unhooked the straps securing Andy in the other safety seat and lifted the two-year-old into her arms. Andy squealed and bounced against her hip as Eve walked with hesitant steps toward their visitor who had squatted before Tanner and was speaking in animated tones with the child.

She watched him stretch to his full height and then pat Tanner's shoulder with one tanned hand before turning dark brown eyes to her and the child in her arms. His radiant smile and flash of perfect white teeth made her heart leap, but then an expression she could describe only as utter bewilderment crossed his face as he stared at Andy.

He reached out and fingered a delicate dark curl before moving his hand to touch the thin cotton fabric of the child's lacy sundress. "Andy?"

"That's my little sister, Mr. Nunez." Tanner hopped up and down near them. "We call her Andy. She's okay, but she squeals sometimes and gets into my things."

"Andy is a girl?" Andres Nunez's brown eyes had widened into huge, round spheres of astonishment. "But I thought I had a son."

"No, Mr. Nunez." Eve shook her head. It was obvious that the poor man was confused, but that was not her fault. If he had taken a little more interest in his child, the misunderstanding could have been cleared up long before the little girl had celebrated her second birthday. "You have a daughter."

Eve felt herself relax a small degree as Andy grinned. She looked up at the tall stranger, still staring in silence. "Meet Rosita Andrea Roberts, Mr. Nunez."

She watched his expression soften as he stroked the child's tiny head and followed Andy's energetic movements with his eyes. His daughter had always been an adorable, captivating child. Eve had no doubt that the little girl would soon manage to pull the emotional strings of even a disinterested, absentee father like Andres Nunez.

Andy's dark eyes sparkled with childlike delight as she grinned at the stranger and then turned to Eve. "I hungry, Mommy."

"Me too." Tanner pulled on Andres' arm. "Mom always makes a special breakfast on Sunday after church. Today, we're having pancakes and sausage."

The little boy's blue eyes glistened with obvious anticipation as he tilted his head to look up at the man standing beside him. "Can you stay and eat with us, Mr. Nunez?"

Eve saw her son turn expectant eyes to her. "Can he, Mom? I mean, may he? We always have lots of food."

She smiled and tried to ignore the quivering sensation in her stomach at the thought of sharing a meal with a man she did not know. She had not yet had time to sort out all of her feelings about Andres Nunez being there in her life and spending time with her family; but, at the same moment, she thought she had no choice except to invite him to breakfast. It was the hospitable and polite thing to do.

"Of course, Mr. Nunez is welcome to join us. Now, go change out of your good clothes."

Tanner wrinkled his nose but conceded to her instructions and, reaching for the railing, began ascending the stairs to the house. Eve kissed the top of Andy's curly head and smiled at the little girl. "You can have a snack, sweetheart, while I get things ready."

She turned her gaze to the tall man standing beside her. "We're just getting home from church so it'll take me about thirty minutes to prepare breakfast."

As he lifted a long, tanned arm and dragged a hand through his dark hair, she noticed that he was wearing the same clothes he had worn the previous night. Tiny creases fanned out from the corners of his brown eyes that were outlined on the bottom edges with dark circles. The sight of the deep, horizontal lines etched across his forehead and his tired, drawn face touched her heart despite the uneasiness his presence created.

"I'm afraid I'm not very presentable." He gave her a slight smile as he fingered the ruffle at the hem of Andy's dress. "I should have planned better, I guess, when I decided to come to Buxton. After I left here last night, I was too late to get a room anywhere on the island. I would have had to go all the way back to Nags Head, but after the long drive from Washington, I was tired and didn't trust myself to stay awake. I pulled off at a beach parking area on the other side of the village for the night."

"You slept in your car?" Pangs of guilt stabbed in Eve's stomach as she recalled her unequivocal order that he leave her house until the following day. She had not invited him in to sit down or to have a cold drink. In fact, she had been so nervous about his unannounced arrival that she had not even opened the door to him.

He shook his head. "Not very well. I couldn't stretch out my legs, and a couple of mosquitoes that eluded my swats were determined to buzz near my ears for hours. I finally gave up the idea of trying to sleep and took a walk along the beach."

Shame heated her cheeks as she stared into his tired, brown eyes. "Oh, Mr. Nunez, I'm so sorry."

A tentative grin tugged at the corners of his mouth and eased her embarrassment. "Please, it's Andres, and there's no reason for you to apologize. I didn't realize that this island was such a popular vacation place, and I'd forgotten it was a holiday weekend."

With one hand, he rubbed the growth of beard on his chin. "If I could use your bathroom to clean up and change my clothes—"

"Yes, yes, of course, Mr.—" She stopped and felt her cheeks burn again. "I mean, Andres. Right this way."

After he retrieved a duffel bag from the trunk of his sports car, he followed her up the wide wooden steps that led to the entrance of the cottage. As they reached the top, she stood aside on the natural finished wrap-around deck to allow him to enter through the door behind which he had spoken to her the previous night. She noticed that he was limping, seeming to favor his left leg, and clutching the railing for support before squaring his shoulders and stepping into the combination laundry room and hallway leading to the galley kitchen.

Beads of perspiration glistened along his tanned forehead as he leaned against the washer. Concern swept over Eve as she watched him inhale deep breaths of air. She saw him strain to hide his obvious pain.

"How about something cold to drink?" She smiled,

feeling a need to ease his discomfort despite her own misgivings regarding his presence there. Andy bounced in her arms and grinned at the handsome stranger.

The strand of dark hair had fallen across his damp forehead once again, and he pushed it back with his hand. "Yes, thanks, as soon as I change."

"The bathroom is right through that door." She pointed to his right. "There are fresh towels and wash-cloths in the cabinet above the sink. I'm afraid there's no tub, only a shower stall. If you prefer a bath, you're welcome to use the other bathroom just down the hall."

"No, a shower is fine. I appreciate your hospitality, Mrs. Bennett. Your husband won't mind, I hope."

"Husband?" His words caught her by surprise. "Oh, no. Edwin died seven years ago."

When Andres emerged from the bathroom twenty minutes later, aromas of breakfast preparations filled his breath and made his mouth water. How long had it been since he had eaten a home-cooked meal?

As he passed through the galley kitchen to the small, adjacent dining area with wide sliding doors that over-looked the calm waters of the canal leading to the sound between Hatteras Island and the mainland of North Carolina, he observed Eve Bennett leaning over the round, white table toward Andy, who was strapped in a highchair. The sight of the dark, curly haired child caused a large lump to grow in his throat. The soft, loose locks bounced around her little head as she giggled at something Eve said.

Rosita Andrea Roberts. His daughter. Cheryl had not allowed her ill feelings for him and his career to dissipate enough to give the child his last name, but she had conceded to first and middle names of Spanish origin, even going so far as using a feminine form of his own given name.

He watched the child stuff a piece of purple grape into her mouth. Her delicate facial features reminded him of Cheryl, but Andy's olive-toned skin, high cheekbones, and the abundance of thick, dark hair were all Nunez family traits. In the little girl's ready smile, he saw his grandmother, and his heart swelled.

Eve Bennett straightened, and she lifted green eyes that widened in apparent surprise as she saw him. Her smile was tentative and did not spread beyond her mouth. The fingers of one of her hands crept to the round neckline of her simple cotton dress and played with the edge of fabric as she moistened her lips with the tip of her tongue.

"Andres. I hope you found everything you needed."

Approaching the table, he smiled before squatting next to Andy's chair. "Yes, thank you. Sometimes I forget what a luxury it is to take a daily shower."

Her green eyes widened. "Luxury?"

"Without the interruptions of insurgent gunfire or the threat of bombs."

He watched an expression of shock cover her pretty,

pale face as she listened to his explanation. Her little nose sprinkled with light freckles wrinkled at him, and he wished he had chosen his words with more care.

She inhaled a deep breath. "We live a very peaceful existence here on Hatteras Island. I'm happy to say that showers are not luxuries, and high winds and tropical storms are the only events that may interrupt them by knocking out the electric power."

He accepted a piece of purple grape from Andy and marveled at the difference just a few days had made in his life. Baghdad, sniper fire, and his job as a correspondent seemed far, far away as he watched his little daughter clap her tiny hands and offer him another piece of fruit.

A clomping sound of approaching footsteps made Andres turn his head to see Eve Bennett's son sauntering into the dining area toward him. The child wore crisp, clean blue jeans with a suede vest over a long-sleeved shirt decorated with silver snaps down the front and on the cuffs. On his feet, he had brown leather boots with pointed toes and silver spurs. Hiding his blond head was an enormous Stetson hat.

Andres held out his right hand to the child. "Well, howdy, partner. Heading out on the range after breakfast?"

Tanner's blue eyes sparkled as he grinned. "Hey, you sound just like John Wayne. Isn't he great? Mom, can we—I mean—may Mr. Nunez and I watch a Western movie?"

From her place at the kitchen counter, his mother shook her head. "Not now. I need your help getting breakfast ready. Please take off your hat, wash your hands, and come squeeze the oranges for juice."

"Aw, Mom." The child's disappointment was obvious in his downcast expression. "The Duke's my hero. Do you like John Wayne too, Mr. Nunez?"

Andres nodded. "He was an exceptional actor. Maybe we could watch one of his movies later." He winked at Tanner. "Right now, you'd better do as your mother says, *mi charro*."

"Me chaddo?" The little boy wrinkled his nose. "What did you call me?"

After smiling at Andy, he rose and took Tanner's hand and then pulled a chair to the counter. "*Mi charro* means "my little cowboy." My grandfather used to call me that."

Tanner kneeled on the chair and washed before Andres handed him an orange half and slid the glass juicer within the child's reach. Tanner squeezed an amazing amount of pulpy liquid from the fruit. Next, he waited while Andres lifted the glass receptacle and poured the juice into a nearby pitcher before giving Tanner another orange half. Then together they repeated the process.

"Did your grandpa call you *mi charro* because you liked to dress like a cowboy?"

Andres nodded. "I still do when I'm home."

"You do? Really?"

"I always wear my boots and hat and jeans when I'm going to ride."

Tanner stopped squeezing to stare up at him. "You ride? Horses? Do you have a horse of your own, Mr. Nunez?"

"I have many at my family's ranch."

"You have a ranch? Hey, Mom, did you hear that? Mr. Nunez has a ranch and horses." With vigor, the little boy squeezed another orange. "Wow, a real ranch with real horses. Can we go visit, Mom?"

"Tanner, you know it's not polite to invite yourself to someone's house."

Andres watched Eve Bennett open the oven door as an enticing aroma of cinnamon and vanilla filled the kitchen. Removing a pan of plump golden muffins, she set the timer on the counter and wiped her hands on the front of her plain white apron tied around her small waist. Waves of auburn hair brushed her slender shoulders as she placed a hand on her son's back.

"How's the juice coming? You can set the table when you're done."

Andres marveled at the ease and grace with which the petite, cheerful mother moved around the galley kitchen. First, she smiled at her son. Next, she retrieved pieces of grapes from the floor around Andy's chair and kissed the child's head. Then she returned to the counter where she began mixing a combination of dried herbs and spices in a bowl and added ground meat from the refrigerator.

The smells of cooking and baking combined with the sounds of the little family preparing breakfast caused Andres' mind to wander for a moment to thoughts of sharing such an ordinary life with a woman he loved and children of his own. Once he'd had a dream like that. What happened to that vision of a typical family and home life? At what point had he given up that idea in order to follow his career?

The image of Cheryl, angry and crying and demanding he leave his job, created a familiar feeling of disillusionment that he wanted to ignore. Today, there was no future and no past. There was just now, and he wanted to spend it getting to know the curly haired child who was his daughter. He had no plans beyond the next few hours.

Feeling a tug on his arm, Andres realized that Eve Bennett's young son had been speaking to him. He pulled himself from the uncomfortable memories and smiled down at the little boy with a trail of freckles over the bridge of his small nose, just like his mother's.

"Do you wear a hat and a vest too, Mr. Nunez?"

Andres took a handful of silverware from Tanner and followed the child to the table. Andy squealed and clapped her hands about some secret, two-year-old delight.

Patting the little girl's head, he turned to Tanner. "Yes, but my vests were never as nice as yours. You look like a genuine Western rancher."

The blond boy's face glowed with obvious pride. "Mom made my cowboy suit. She's a good sewer."

Andres looked across the room and met Eve Bennett's eyes. Her face flushed as he smiled. "Indeed she is. You are very lucky to have such a talented mother."

With her hands, she formed ground pork into patties and placed them in a heated frying pan on the stove. "I'm afraid you're going to be too hot in those clothes today, Tanner. The temperature is supposed to reach one hundred degrees by noon."

The child set four ceramic plates around the edge of the round table and wrinkled his nose. "But we're going to Buxton Woods. If I can't ride the horses, I want them to see my cowboy outfit, anyway. Please, Mom."

"We may have to change our plans. Mr. Nunez has come to spend the day with Andy. I'm not sure he'll want to go hiking with us."

Tanner tipped his head and sent Andres a pleading look. "Will you come with us? You and Andy can watch the turtles. She likes that. And you can see the horses. There are great horses at the stables there. You said you like horses, right, Mr. Nunez?"

With a warm smile on her face, Eve stepped into the dining area and slipped an arm around her son's small shoulders. "You're so persistent this morning. You haven't even given our guest a chance to answer." She lifted bright green eyes to Andres. "Before you called, we had made plans to hike along a nearby nature trail today."

Tanner grabbed Andres' hand. "Buxton Woods is a maritime forest. That means it's near the ocean. There's a trail that goes all the way to Frisco, but that's too far to walk when it's hot, Mom says." The little boy's blue eyes sparkled. "I like the pond best, with all of the tadpoles and crawfish and salamanders. You'll come, won't you, Mr. Nunez? Oh, it'll be so fun, and you can see the horses."

Tanner was still chattering without taking a breath as the little group approached the barn at Buxton Stables where the smell of fresh hay and saddle oil filled the hot, humid air of early afternoon. Nothing Eve said or did seemed to curb her son's enthusiasm for the presence of the tall stranger who was disrupting the relaxing day she had planned for her family.

"Just wait till you see the wood ducks and the frogs. And there are so many dragonflies. Do you like dragonflies, Mr. Nunez?"

Andy bounced against Eve's hip as a horse snorted. She smiled and tightened her hold on the child. Andres had asked to carry her, but the little girl still appeared wary of him. Eve did notice, though, that Andy had begun to watch their visitor with interest.

"Let's go say hi to the horses before we start." Tanner grasped Andres' hand and pulled him toward the large wooden structure that sheltered the animals. "Mom says these woods are very special. She says we should enjoy them and protect them because there aren't many maritime forests left in the world."

Andres smiled at Eve as she hurried to keep up with

her son's dash toward a large chestnut mare. "A seam-stress and a conservationist. I am quite impressed, Mrs. Bennett."

Tanner giggled. "She's a nurse too, at my school. That's the only place she's called Mrs. Bennett. Other-wise, she's just Eve. Everybody calls her that."

Andres' dark eyes rose above deep brown eyes and held her gaze. "Everybody?"

She felt a blush warm her cheeks. "Yes, we're not very formal around here."

"Oh, Mom, look. Isn't it the most beautiful horse you've ever seen?"

"Be careful, Tanner."

A young stable hand walked toward them. "This girl's a bit too big for you, sport. We have smaller horses just right for a little guy your size. Would you like me to saddle one up for you?"

The child's blue eyes pleaded with her. "Oh, may I, Mom? Please?"

With the fingers of her free hand, she played with the collar of her sleeveless polo shirt. The idea of her little son riding on top of a large, unfamiliar animal scared her.

She jumped when she felt a hand touch her bare shoulder. "He'll be safe, Eve. I'll walk right along beside the horse and keep a close eye on Tanner. I promise."

She lifted her gaze from her son's blue eyes to the dark brown ones of Andres Nunez. The man's captivat-ing smile made her heart skip a beat.

She swallowed. What was this stranger doing? Tanner was her son, and this man she barely knew was interfering with what she thought was best for her child.

He was there to visit Andy, not to undermine her authority with her own son. The fear that Tanner might be hurt riding a horse combined with growing indignation that the man who was her daughter's father was completely disturbing her normal life. His presence seemed to affect her typically calm and decisive nature.

Tanner seemed to read her hesitancy. "Please, Mom. I'll be careful. I'll do everything Mr. Nunez says. He knows a lot about horses, remember? He has a ranch."

She watched Andres' eyes sparkle. "I've been around horses all my life, Eve."

She shook her head and glanced at her son. "I haven't. They scare me."

His gentle fingers on her shoulder felt comforting. She was not sure she liked the way his smile seemed to mesmerize her and make her forget her responsibilities and her convictions.

"Please, Mom."

Tanner's persistent, pleading voice only added to her confused emotional state, and she sighed. "All right, I guess. You can take a short ride." She held Andres' dark brown eyes in warning. "But you have to be very careful."

Chapter Two

Tanner's short ride turned into over an hour of horse riding instruction and practice with Andres Nunez's quiet patience guiding the little boy as he led the small horse along the sand and shell-covered trails traversing Buxton Woods. Despite Eve's initial reservation concerning her son's request to ride the animal, Andres' vigilance and care and Tanner's obvious delight encouraged her to relax and enjoy the interaction between the two.

Her son certainly did not seem to mind that the man had disrupted their Sunday plans. Eve noticed too, that the more time Andres spent talking and playing with Andy, the more comfortable the little girl appeared to be around him. It was probably inevitable that the children would find Andres' charismatic personality entertaining.

Eve sighed with relief when Tanner finally agreed to return his mount to its stable stall, but only when Andres promised to show him photographs and to recount stories of his boyhood and riding horses on his family's ranch in New Mexico. They spent the next hour and a half strolling along secluded forest paths shaded by a canopy of oak tree branches, low hanging pines, and creeping vines. The familiar sounds of insects buzzing, woodpeckers tapping, and frogs croaking filled Eve's ears and comforted her lingering doubts that inviting a stranger into her house and her life had not been the biggest mistake she had ever made.

"Let me try to take her."

Eve pulled her concentration from the yellow-bellied pond slider disturbing hundreds of tadpoles and hovering insects as it slipped beneath the surface of the water and met deep brown eyes that held her in a mysterious grip she had never before experienced. She swallowed and attempted to steady her breathing.

"You've been carrying the child for too long without a break, and she's refusing to sit in the stroller. So why don't you let me try? Holding a bouncing, wiggling little person must be exhausting for you."

He leaned down and rubbed his daughter's cheek with his fingertips, and the little girl giggled and hid her curly head against Eve's bare shoulder while still sneaking a glance at the man who seemed to hold her interest more keenly than the turtles sliding into the water.

"Silly, Mister," she said in her sweet, soft voice.

"It's not just *Mister*, Andy. It's *Mr. Nunez.*" Tanner shook his head and turned to Andres. "She's learning to talk, and she still makes a lot of mistakes."

Eve watched Andres finger one of Andy's curls as he winked at Tanner. "Andy's lucky she has a big brother like you to help her."

Her son beamed with pride, straightened his shoulders, and puffed out his small chest. "Come on, Andy. Mr. Nunez wants to hold you. He's a very nice man. See?"

Andy's eyes followed Tanner's hand as the little boy reached out and patted Andres' tanned forearm. "He wants to give Mom a break. She never gets one from taking care of you."

The child in Eve's arms struggled against her hold. "I walk, Mommy. I walk."

Eve smiled and shook her head. "You'd like that, wouldn't you?" Trying to hide her hesitancy with a laugh, she placed the child in Andres' outstretched arms. She ignored the tumbling in her stomach as she watched Andy flash her father a smile of apparent acceptance.

"Hold on tight." Tanner hopped up and down at the tall man's side. "If you let her go, we'll be chasing her all over the woods. Andy loves to run!"

Eve inhaled a deep breath as they strolled along the quiet path of tangled wild grape and holly bushes. An individual passing them would probably think they were a family out enjoying a Sunday afternoon, but that was not true.

They were not a family. Andres Nunez was a

stranger, although Eve could not deny the powerful effect his presence had begun to have on her and her children in just a few hours. She felt as though she were slipping into unknown territory. It felt as if she were being pulled underneath the surface of the ocean by a powerful wave. She was struggling to keep her head above the water, just as she was trying to stop Andres from changing the only life she knew.

"I'm thirsty, Mom."

Tanner slipped his small hand into Eve's as she tried to catch up with Andres' long stride. Was he limping? Perspiration beaded across his tanned forehead, and she thought he appeared tired.

Andy squealed and bounced against his side. One tiny finger reached for the green and black dragonfly that had landed on her father's broad shoulder.

"I need some water." Tanner repeated his request for a drink in a more urgent tone than he had used a few moments before then.

"Me too." Andy echoed her brother's declaration as she pressed her palm against Andres' cheek.

The man's smile eased the discomfort Eve's thoughts had evoked. Andy seemed to like the man, and he appeared to be growing fond of his daughter.

"Mom."

"Yes, yes, Tanner. You're thirsty." She looked down at him. "There are some bottles of water in the cooler in the car. We probably should be getting back home. Andy needs her nap."

"A nap? Oh, Mom, she doesn't even look tired to me."

Eve followed her son's gaze to Andy, who had twisted around her tiny fingers the silver chain that hung from Andres' neck. The child studied the round medallion on it with intense interest. "Pretty necklace, Mister Noo-Noo."

"Not *Noo-Noo*, you silly girl." Tanner shook his head. "His name is *Nu-nez*." He raised his blue eyes to Andres. "She acts like such a baby sometimes."

Andres' chuckle made Eve's heart jump before resuming its normal rhythm. She watched as another smile lit up his handsome face, accenting his narrow jaw, high cheekbones, and the tiny lines fanning out from the corners of his deep brown eyes.

"Be patient, *mi charro*. Soon she will be speaking clearly and correctly and telling *you* how to say things."

"Telling *me*?"

He nodded. "I bet it won't be long before she'll be correcting how you speak and what you do and everything. Women like to take charge."

"They do?"

"Oh, yes. They tell men what to do and how to live and what to say." Andres met Eve's gaze over Andy's curly head, and his eyes sparkled with obvious mischief. "They think that we need their help and that they have to take care of us."

Tanner nodded his blond head as though he were in complete agreement with Andres Nunez. "Oh, I get it. You mean that women are bossy, right?"

Eve wanted to be angry as she watched a grin tug at the corners of the tanned man's mouth, but the awe she saw in her son's eyes stopped her from disagreeing with Andres. She would wait to do that when her son was not presence.

"Absolutely, *mi charro*. We men need to stick together."

"While Andy takes her nap, Mr. Nunez and I can go fishing." Tanner turned as he reached the porch surrounding the cottage as Andres, with Andy in his arms, followed Eve up the wooden steps to the front door. "We still have some bait in the refrigerator, don't we, Mom?"

The hot, humid air pressed against Eve's skin causing her sleeveless polo shirt and cotton walking shorts to cling to her arms and legs. Uncomfortable and irritable, she pushed back a strand of hair that had worked its way out of the elastic band at her nape.

"I'm sure Mr. Nunez has other plans, Tanner." In fact, she hoped he would leave. She needed some time to sit down and relax without the dark eyes of the tall, Latin man scrutinizing every move she made.

Reaching the top of the stairs, she unlocked the door and stepped into the coolness of the air-conditioned house. Had the sudden change in temperature made her shiver, or was Andres' nearness right behind her causing her to shudder with an intense awareness that energized her raw nerves?

When she turned and held her arms out to take the sleeping child from him, Andres' face broke into a captivating smile. "Just point the way, and I'll put her down."

She wanted to protest, but instead, she nodded and led him through the hallway to Andy's bedroom. She watched his muscles expand and contract as he placed the little girl with gentle, careful movements onto the lower bunk and covered her tiny sleeping body with a light blanket draped over the footboard.

Eve felt his eyes on her as she switched on the power of one baby monitor on the nearby bed stand and clipped the other one to the waistband of her shorts. They stepped from the room, and Andres pulled the door closed.

"How long will she sleep?"

His quiet question so close to her ear made her tremble. The warmth of his breath against her cheek took away her breath for a few moments.

"Um, probably a couple of hours. The hike in the woods really tired her out." She tipped her head and watched him nod.

"Me too." He lifted a long arm and pushed the thick rebel strand of hair back from his forehead. "It's been years since I have spent that much time with children. Their energy supply seems limitless."

"There you are, Mr. Nunez." Tanner rushed toward them as he waved a small, clear plastic bag in the air. "I found the worms. Let's go out and fish off the dock."

Andres eyed the bloodworms resting in a clump of damp, shredding paper bedding at the bottom of the bag in the little boy's hand. "I guess you'll have to teach me what to do, *mi charro*. I grew up on a ranch, and I've never caught a fish in my life."

"Tanner, Mr. Nunez is tired. Put those worms away—"

The child's smile faded, and his small shoulders slumped. "Aw, Mom—"

Andres rested his hand on her back and smiled at her. "If you don't mind, I would like to try fishing. I am not too tired to learn a few tips from a pro like Tanner."

Eve tried to ignore the gentle touch of his hand on the back of her polo shirt. No, he could not be asking to stay. She needed to recuperate from the devastating effect of his presence.

Tanner squealed, and she swallowed the verbal objection on the tip of her tongue. She nodded her reluctant consent as Andres grinned.

"Oh, this'll be so fun. I'll get the poles, and we'll catch some croakers and maybe some sea trout. Do you like trout, Mr. Nunez?"

She watched the tall, handsome man nod and ruffle Tanner's blond hair. "Yes, I like to eat trout. I am just not sure about catching them. Before we head out to the dock, though, I'd like you to start calling me Andres."

Her son grinned. "Sure, Andres. And you can call me *charro* because I'm like a cowboy in Argentina. I even know how to ride a horse now."

"That's right." He winked at Eve. "Maybe someday, we can get your mother to try."

"Oh, that's a good joke, Andres. Mom's a scaredy cat."

"Maybe you and I can convince her that there is nothing to be afraid of, that life is more fun when you take a few risks."

Tanner's expression held obvious skepticism, and he shook his head. "You can try, I guess."

"We will have to think of a plan to help her." Andres patted the child's shoulder. "Now, you are going to show me how to fish, and later, after Andy wakes up from her nap, I would like to buy you dinner."

"Sure. Let's have pizza."

"I thought we would go out to eat. On my drive here this morning, I passed a place with a deck overlooking the water. Do you know which one I'm talking about?"

"The big restaurant with the tall pole next to the parking lot?"

"That's it."

"The Masthead. We've never gone there, have we, Mom?"

"That's because it's too expensive." Eve set a hand on her son's other shoulder. "I'm afraid we couldn't impose on you like that, Andres."

The man's brown eyes held a warmth that reached out and touched her heart. "I've been imposing on you and your family all day. Allow me to repay your hospitality."

She managed a smile, yet she did not feel the friendliness and gratitude such an expression was supposed to represent. The last thing she wanted to do was spend more time with Andres Nunez, especially at one of the nicest places on Hatteras Island with two young children who did not appreciate the expense he would be making.

She inhaled a long, deep breath. "That's very kind of you. The Masthead is a popular restaurant for the tourists, I understand."

He lifted dark eyebrows. "Do you recommend I make reservations?"

"Probably. Both Tanner and Andy get rather impatient when they're hungry."

Andres grinned at her son. "You should see me when I haven't eaten. I'm a bear!" He growled and pretended to claw Tanner with his hand.

The little boy screamed and ran just out of the man's reach. "I hear the croakers calling us, Andres. Let's get out to the dock."

Eve watched Andres Nunez stride toward the sliding glass doors that opened onto the back deck facing the canal that flowed into the water separating Hatteras Island from the mainland of North Carolina. Again she noticed the unmistakable limp. She did not want to be interested, and yet she could not disregard the questions she had concerning the tall, Latin man who was quickly becoming a part of her life.

Eve allowed her gaze to roam around the wide outdoor deck filled with patrons of The Masthead restaurant. Tables were spaced far enough apart to ensure privacy for the couples and small family groups dining in the idyllic setting overlooking the breathtaking rays of the evening sun that reflected across the still waters on Pamlico Sound.

"What a gorgeous view."

Her heart fluttered when she heard Andres' quiet voice, and she turned to meet his dark brown eyes. From his seat on the other side of the table, he smiled.

"How did you ever discover such a wonderful island vacation spot?"

Eve held a large glass of ice water to Andy's mouth so the little girl could take a drink. "I didn't. My parents have been coming to Hatteras Island every summer since they spent their honeymoon here thirty years ago."

She felt his eyes on her as she wiped Andy's mouth with a linen napkin and then handed the child a small board book. When the little girl began to flip through the thick pages, Eve turned her attention back to Andres. "The cottage we're staying in belongs to them."

"Your parents are not here right now, then?"

She shook her head. "My sister's having her second baby soon so Dad and Mom flew to Indiana to be with her and her family. They plan to be here for the whole month of August if everything goes okay with the new baby's delivery."

He pushed aside the strand of dark hair that refused to stay off his forehead and leaned back in his chair. Even when he was sitting, he still looked very tall.

She noticed that although he appeared to hide how he felt, the dark circles under his eyes and the drawn expression on his face told her he was tired. The poor man had slept in his car at the beach all night. Guilt nagged at her.

She watched him add an *O* to the tic-tac-toe grid on the slip of paper she had given Tanner to write on while they waited for their food to arrive before he looked across the table at her again. "As a school nurse, you get summers off from work?"

"I won!" Tanner drew a line through his row of *X*s and grinned in triumph. "Let's play again."

"I hungry, Mommy." Andy's declaration was accompanied by a muffled banging noise as the little girl tapped a spoon on the linen tablecloth.

"Shh, sweetie." Eve removed the utensil from the child's grip as she patted Andy's curly head. "I have a snack for you in my purse."

She pulled a clear plastic bag filled with round yellow puffs of corn breakfast cereal and opened it. Andy watched in sudden interest as Eve set a handful of pieces on the table within the child's reach.

The little girl trapped a sphere of corn cereal between her tiny thumb and forefinger and then popped it into her mouth. She repeated the action as Eve turned back to Andres.

"Yes, I take summers off to spend time with Tanner and Andy. We came down from Arlington as soon as school finished for the year. Not everyone in my family comes to Hatteras at once, but all of my siblings and their spouses and children try to spend at least a week or two here during the summer months."

"You have a large family?"

"Three brothers and two sisters. All married, all with kids."

Andres whistled softly. "And they all fit in that little cottage?"

Eve shook her head. "Tanner, Andy, and I stay there with Mom and Dad. The rest of them rent houses nearby. I'm sure you've noticed that there are many vacation places for rent on the island. Tourism is a big business in the Outer Banks area although our neighborhood is still quite private. Only a few places are rental homes."

"Like Mr. and Mrs. Wetmore's house next door." Tanner pushed the piece of paper toward Andres. "Your turn."

Eve nodded. "Our neighbors are an elderly couple who moved here from Alaska. Three years ago they decided to move back to Fairbanks to stay with family during the summer. They come back to Hatteras Island after the hurricane season is over every year."

"So your neighbors rent their house while they are gone?"

"I'm not sure how committed they are to the idea of renting. Mr. and Mrs. Wetmore have had their place listed for three summers now, and it's still vacant. I assume that they are asking an extremely high weekly rate."

"Mr. Wetmore says their house costs a lot because it has a baby pool and a rope bridge."

Eve watched Andres turn wide, questioning eyes to her son. "Baby pool?"

"A hot tub on the third-floor balcony," she explained.

"And a bridge that goes all the way across the living room way up high." Tanner wrinkled his nose. "But Mom won't let me cross it, even with Mr. Wetmore right there."

"It's a swinging bridge of wooden slats suspended by a system of ropes and knots across the cathedral ceiling of the main living room. Just looking at it makes me dizzy."

"Mom walked across it lots of times when she was a little girl, but now she won't let me do it even once."

She patted her son's arm. "I'm much smarter now and much more careful."

"And not as much fun."

She saw Andres grin at Tanner's comment as the little boy bent his blond head and studied the tic-tac-toe move his opponent had just made. "I think I might beat you again."

"Put the game away now, and let Andres wait for his dinner in peace."

With obvious reluctance, Tanner folded the paper and set the pen on the top of it. His blue eyes roamed around the table and settled on Andy.

"Hey, how come she gets to eat? I want some cereal too."

"You're big enough to wait."

"Aw, Mom, I'm hungry."

Eve set another handful of cereal in front of Andy and then filled Tanner's outstretched hand with corn puffs. "Now, be patient. Our food will be coming soon."

"Want some?"

Andres accepted pieces of cereal from Tanner and popped them into his mouth. Studying his profile, Eve saw his strong, narrow jaw flex as he chewed. His bronze cheeks moved when he swallowed.

"Mm, those were good." Tanner grinned. "Toss me some more, Mom."

Before she had a chance to respond, Andres picked up a pale yellow puff on the table in front of Andy and lobbed the cereal toward her son. Reacting with smoothness and skill, Tanner caught it in his hand and giggled in triumph.

Eve watched in growing irritation as the little boy tossed the cereal ball back to Andres. In an attempt to be discreet, she leaned across the table toward them. "Stop that right now! You know better, Tanner."

She kept her voice low, but she felt her face flush with annoyance and embarrassment. The expressions of enjoyment on the faces to the two offenders frustrated her as she glanced around the deck full of diners to see in any of them had watched the display of inappropriate behavior.

"Stop what?" Andres' mouth curved into a wide smile, and then he tossed a piece of cereal in her direction.

Without thinking, she caught the yellow ball in her fist. Narrowing her eyes, she glared at him as Tanner and Andy clapped.

"Good catch, Mom."

Eve frowned at her son and then returned her attention to the attractive, tanned man seated across from her. She watched his appealing smile fade as he set a large hand on Tanner's shoulder.

"Your mother wants us to use our manners, *mi charro.* It is always important to women that the men around them act politely and properly."

The little boy rolled his eyes. "You mean they like to boss us?"

Eve held her temper in check as a grin pulled at the corners of Andres' appealing mouth. She watched him turn with a patronizing look of contrition on his handsome face.

"We are very sorry, Eve."

"Yes. Sorry, Mom."

"Please accept our sincere apologies even though we were just having fun."

She could barely hear his last words as he whispered them across the table to her. She formed an angry retort in her mind, but fortunately their server arrived with their dinners at that moment.

Boy, are you lucky, mister. The words tumbled over

her tongue as she cut linguini with cheese sauce into little pieces on a plate in front of Andy. *Our server saved you from a good scolding.*

Who did Andres Nunez think he was, anyway? First he showed up unannounced late at night demanding to see Andy. Then he pushed his way into their Sunday plans, and next he threw cereal with her son in one of the island's most prestigious restaurants.

As she turned to offer Tanner assistance with his fish and chips meal, her heated thoughts faded from her mind. From across the table, she watched Andres cut her son's batter dipped haddock and then spoon ketchup from a crystal condiment jar onto the child's deep-fried potatoes.

As he leaned toward Tanner, his dark head contrasted with her son's blond one. Their voices were low and too quiet to hear, but she could see by the smiles on their faces that the two were sharing a pleasant and amusing conversation.

The picture of Andres Nunez talking with her son during dinner was still etched in her mind a few hours later when Eve tucked the little boy into his carved oak bed. After tossing some plastic action figures into the stenciled crate on the floor, she smoothed the sheet under his chin and kissed his forehead.

"Mom?"

"Yes?"

"When we adopt Andy, will Andres be my dad too?"

Eve felt as though a band tightened around her heart. "You have a father, Tanner."

"I know I *did* have one, but I don't remember him, and you said he died before I was born." The little boy shook his head. "It's just not fair, Mom."

"What's not?"

"That Andy has a great dad like Andres and I don't. I want him to be my dad. Can't we ask him to be my dad too?"

Eve sighed. Reaching out her hand, she smoothed blond strands from his face.

He pushed away her hand. "I want a dad who can take me fishing and horseback riding. I want someone who can run and swim and practice baseball with me. Andy's so lucky." Tanner's blue eyes were big and round as they stared up at her from his pillow. "I want Andres to be my dad, Mom."

As Eve switched off his light, she swallowed the dread that had been churning inside of her stomach since Andres Nunez had appeared on her porch the previous night. Closing the door to Tanner's bedroom, she inhaled a deep, steady breath that she hoped would give her courage as she walked to the living room to face the man who had, in less then twenty-four hours, completely disrupted her family's happy, well-ordered life.

As she entered the room furnished with wood-framed couches and chairs and nautical print fabric, Andres turned from where he stood gazing out at the moonlit inlet flowing into Pamlico Sound. In the soft light of the shaded lamp, she saw his brown eyes rise in expectancy as a warm smile brightened the serious lines of his face.

Her fingers were nervous as they played with the rounded neckline of the sleeveless sundress she had worn to dinner, and she inhaled another deep breath. "Would you like some coffee or a cold drink? I could brew some iced tea or squeeze lemons for lemonade."

She glanced around the room trying to figure out what to do next. She suddenly felt awkward and uneasy.

"Coffee would be fine if it is not too much trouble."

His smile broadened and somehow calmed her. She nodded and headed into the kitchen. She tried to ignore the way her heart jumped in her chest and then began to race when she realized he had followed her.

"Thank you for today, Eve."

His words were quiet and edged with a hint of a rich Latin accent that made her think of desert ranches and horses and handsome cowboys tanned in the heat of the Southwestern summer sun. She spooned ground coffee into the filter-lined basket of the coffee maker and slid it into place. After adding water and pushing the power button of the appliance, she turned to face him.

His elbows rested at his sides as he leaned against the counter. The sight of him standing so closely to her caused her heart to race once again. She caught her lower lip between her teeth and chewed with growing nervousness.

"I know it has not been easy for you, having me hang around all day, but I appreciate your kindness."

She swallowed the lump in her throat. "Andy is your daughter."

She watched him stuff his hands into the front pockets of his khaki pants. "I want to be a part of her life, Eve. I want her to know that I am her father."

She recalled Tanner's words as she was tucking him into bed. Andy was not the only child who would be hurt if Andres did not commit himself to his parental obligations.

"Don't you think that would just confuse her? I mean, she's so young. She doesn't understand, and with your job—"

"I have a few weeks off right now."

"A few weeks does not give you time enough to be a father."

"Maybe not, but it could be a start."

She inhaled a deep breath. "If you're going to be a parent, Andres, you have to be committed for a lifetime, not just when it's convenient for you. Being a parent is not a *sometimes* job. You can't expect to come around just when you have a little free time."

"Other parents have careers and responsibilities outside of their family life."

"They also have a home and usually a spouse who is there for the child on a daily basis. You can't just pick and choose when you want to be involved in Andy's life.

She needs a stable home environment. Cheryl asked me to provide that kind of life for her." Eve sighed. "We were neighbors and casual friends. I often took care of Andy when Cheryl was busy. When she decided to write her will, she said she had no close relatives she trusted and asked me if I would be Andy's legal guardian if anything happened to her. You weren't interested in taking Andy."

His brown eyes darkened. "She never told me I had a child."

"Would it have mattered to you?"

She watched a shadow cross his tanned face. "Of course it would have mattered. It *does* matter. Andy is my daughter. My ex-wife gave me no chance to choose, and now you seem to want to take away my choice too."

With care, Eve selected her next words. "I haven't taken away your choices. In fact, I had every intention of cooperating fully with you regarding Andy's legal custody when you came for Cheryl's funeral, but you didn't come."

"I had planned to attend but . . . I was unexpectedly detained."

She nodded. "A few days after the funeral, I received a letter from the State Department and another from the magazine for which you work. Both of them confirmed that you had been a victim of a car bombing in the Middle East and were presumed dead."

She watched him drag a tanned hand through his

hair. A frown on his face created lines across his forehead as his brown eyes leveled on hers.

"I was nearly killed." He reached up and grasped the silver medal that hung around his neck. "I barely remember being captured soon after that by Sunni rebels who were determined to punish me for some incriminating reports I had made about their past terrorist activities."

His tired grin held a sheepish expression. "I divulged too much about the members of their group, and they wanted to get rid of me, but I was fortunate enough to be rescued by some U. S. Marines and taken to an Iraqi clinic where the medical personnel there tried to piece me back together. When I finally woke up and realized where I was, three months had passed since Cheryl's death."

He shook his head. "I missed her funeral. I did not think there was any reason for me to return to Arlington."

"Oh, Andres." Guilt, sadness, and fear gripped her heart. Thoughts of his horrific experiences tumbled through her mind, and Eve swallowed a wave of nausea. She felt empathy growing in her for the man standing in her kitchen. He had survived appalling circumstances that she could neither imagine nor understand. "I'm sorry. I had no idea. I thought you just weren't interested."

He reached across the distance between them in the small galley kitchen and squeezed the fingers of one of her hands. "Cheryl and I may have fallen out of love, or we were, more than likely, never in love at all, but I cared for her. I grieved when she died, and I would have attended her funeral if I had been able to do so. I would have been here for our child too."

His warm touch soothed her distress over the situation. She swallowed again. "Cheryl really never told you about Andy?"

"She never once even hinted about a baby. I had no idea."

"That wasn't right. She shouldn't have kept that kind of news from you. You're Andy's father."

"I am sure my ex-wife thought she was doing the right thing for Andy. She hated my career as a foreign correspondent. I guess she always thought she could persuade me to change professions. Anyway, several months before her accident, she insisted she could not longer live the life we were leading and demanded a divorce. Resisting her would have accomplished nothing, and any feelings I had had for Cheryl had died over the years we spent apart. She could not change me, and I refused to change for her. I signed the papers and sent them back to her lawyer. She never once mentioned a baby."

Eve cleared her throat. "I just always assumed you knew and didn't care."

"I did not learn about Andy's existence until three days ago. I came back home as soon as I could make travel arrangements."

Thoughts raced through Eve's mind as she tried to remember what Cheryl Roberts had told her about her former husband. Even though they had lived next door to each other, Cheryl had actually shared very little about her personal life.

Eve attempted to put herself in Andres' position for a moment. If he was telling the truth, and she had no reason to doubt him, he had very good cause to be upset. He had a two-year-old daughter he did not know. Receiving the news of her existence must have been shocking to him.

She reached for his other hand and smiled up at him. "I apologize for any part I may have played in the deception. Andy is your daughter. Cheryl was clear about that fact. You are named on Andy's birth certificate as her father. I'm sure we'll be able to work out a plan for you to take part in Andy's life."

"I understand you have adopted my daughter."

Eve looked up into his deep brown eyes. "When you were declared legally dead, I went ahead with the required proceedings. Andy needed a family." She inhaled a long breath. "Her adoption should be finalized before the end of the summer."

He nodded. "The child is obviously quite attached to you, and you take wonderful care of her. I would like to propose a type of joint custody agreement."

"Of course, Andres. She is your child." She chewed her lower lip.

"What is it?"

"Well, Andy's last name . . . I was going to change it

to Bennett, but now I think it should be Nunez. Your daughter should have your name."

His smile was tentative. "Yes, I think so too."

The aroma of fresh-brewed coffee wafted through the air, and Eve pulled her trembling hands away from him. She poured two cups of the rich, dark, decaffeinated liquid. Swallowing, she forced a smile. "Cream and sugar?"

He sighed. "No, just black, thanks." He accepted the mug of steaming drink and strode to the table in the dining area.

Following him, Eve could not help but see the noticeable limp of his left leg. She watched him lower himself into a chair as pain appeared to tighten the muscles of his face.

"You're hurting." She took a seat adjacent to him. "What's wrong?"

He played with the ceramic handle of his coffee mug before lifting brown eyes to look at her. "I guess I have not done a very good job of hiding it."

"I've noticed that your left leg has been giving you trouble off and on all day."

He nodded. "It is a souvenir from that last car bomb."

She felt her eyes widen at his words. "Last one? There have been more?"

He met her gaze and reached for the medal around his neck. "Saint Isidore always looks after me, but my leg got in the way and took a little damage that time." A smile accompanied his sheepish expression. "The doctors say with proper rest and physical therapy, I may even walk normally again."

"So, why aren't you resting and getting the treatment you need?"

"Uh-oh. Is that disapproval I hear in your voice, Nurse Bennett?"

She smiled in spite of her irritation that he was not taking care of himself. "I don't stop being a nurse just because I'm on vacation. Seriously, though, you need to give yourself time to heal."

He nodded over the rim of his coffee mug. "I'm supposed to use a cane."

"A cane? We walked miles on the Buxton Woods trails this afternoon. You should have said something. I would have found a cane for you to use."

His look was full of guilt. "I have one in my car."

"Then why didn't you use it?"

"I am afraid to admit that my male vanity prevented me from doing what was right. I guess you should know that I am a proud man, Eve."

She rolled her eyes at him. "You shouldn't have carried Andy all that way or led Tanner around on the horse. My goodness, Andres. I can't stand by and let you be so cavalier about your health."

He raised his eyebrows above brown eyes full of mischief. "I think Tanner is right. You *are* bossy."

Despite his playful tone, Eve squared her shoulders. "My son said no such thing. You're the one filling him with ideas that women like to be in charge and enjoy telling men what to do."

He grinned. "Well, don't they?"

She considered his question. "Only when we think certain men are making poor decisions. Some men need a little guidance and direction."

He finished his coffee. "Is that what you think I need, Nurse Bennett? A bit of direction in my life?"

His intent gaze made her mouth turn dry, and she took a quick drink of her own coffee. Swallowing, she pulled her eyes from his.

She watched him stretch his long arms above his head. "Well, I should get going. I have a long trip back to Washington tonight."

"You look too tired to drive all that way. Maybe you should stay in Buxton tonight and head up in the morning."

"There's no hotel room available in the whole village, and there won't be for a couple more days. I already checked." He reached across the table and squeezed her hand. "If I get tired, I'll just find a place to pull off the road and sleep for a while. I have a meeting with my editor tomorrow morning and an appointment with an orthopedic specialist in the afternoon. I should be able to leave Washington by five or so."

"Turn around and drive right back? Andres, that's crazy!"

"I don't want Andy to forget who I am."

"If you die in a car crash, she'll never know you at all."

He smiled at her as he grasped the sterling silver medal on the chain around his neck. "I'll be back. I promise. I don't die easily."

Chapter Three

"The house is quite large, almost too big for one occupant. Are you sure you wouldn't like to look at some smaller rental options. Mr. Nunez? There are several furnished cottages available farther down on the sound side of the island."

Andres pulled his eyes away from the treetop view of Pamlico Sound and the surrounding residential neighborhood just outside of Buxton, North Carolina, as he stood on the shaded fourth-floor porch of the well-maintained cedar-sided home. He smiled at the real estate agent standing beside him.

Shoving his free hand into the front pocket of his pants, he shook his head. "No, this place is large, but I like it. After living in hotel rooms, dusty tents, and dingy bunkers for the past three years, I look forward to the idea of wandering around in several stories of empty rooms with lots of windows and open space."

With apparent surprise, the tall, slender woman stared at him. "Tents and bunkers? I thought you said you're a journalist."

"I am. A foreign correspondent for a Washington-based news magazine. I've been covering political unrest and terrorist activity in the Middle East. Accommodations are not always the most comfortable or welcoming."

"Well, I'm sure you'll find the Wetmore place extremely peaceful. This neighborhood is generally quiet and free of most of the tourist traffic out on the main road. The majority of the people who live here are either full-time or summer residents who choose not to rent their homes. In fact, my husband and I live just a little farther down on the canal from here."

Although Andres was not particularly interested in the details realtors used to persuade people to enter into rental agreements for local vacation homes, the agent seemed insistent about presenting to him all the benefits of living in that particular neighborhood. He shifted his weight against the support of his cane and forced his mind to focus on her rather than on the pretty, auburn-haired woman next door who was his temporary neighbor and the guardian of his little girl.

With difficulty, he pushed the pleasant image of her freckle-flecked nose and bright, warm smile from his thoughts. Maybe moving into the house beside Eve Bennett's was not such a good idea after all.

"Neil and Betty Wetmore had enjoyed living on the Outer Banks for years before they were persuaded by their children to move back to their home state of Alaska where the elderly couple live near their family."

The realtor smiled. "Their children want Neil and Betty to sell this house and move back to Fairbanks permanently. But they are not quite ready to do that yet. However, they have agreed to rent the house under certain conditions while they are gone."

"And do I meet those conditions, Mrs. Halsey?"

"Please, it's Lisa; and yes, you have, I'm happy to say. The Wetmores insist on a month commitment rather than the typical weekly contract. In addition, they request that the lessee pay a security deposit equal to the amount of the four-week stay."

She moved her leather portfolio from one hand to the other. "Usually only oceanfront owners in the northern part of the Outer Banks are able to charge such an exorbitant rent. As I understand, you will be traveling back and forth to Washington two or three times a week and are not even sure if you will be able to stay the whole month. I can't help wondering why you would choose this house when there are so many more affordable ones available."

Trying to listen, Andres allowed his gaze to wander again to the house to his right nestled among a grove of cedar and pine trees just a few hundred feet from the calm water of the small inlet leading to Pamlico Sound. Movement on the wraparound porch captured his attention as a thin boy wearing a huge Stetson hat and cowboy boots opened the sliding glass door and stepped outdoors. He watched the child take a seat on the bench of the wooden picnic table.

Andres raised his eyebrows to the real estate agent. "I want this house, not a smaller one or a cheaper one. I like this particular house. I'm prepared to pay the deposit and rental fees right now. Do we have a deal?"

If Lisa Halsey was surprised by the firmness of his decision, she did not demonstrate it. Instead, she pulled some forms from the leather portfolio in her hand and gave him a wide smile. "Of course, Mr. Nunez. I'll just need your signature on a few papers. Shall we go inside and get out of the heat? You look as though you need to sit down. Is your injury giving you some trouble?"

With reluctance, he took one last glance at Tanner Bennett playing on the porch at the house next door and then followed Lisa Halsey into the large beach house he was about to rent. Anticipation mixed with apprehension as he contemplated the decisions he had already made that had affected his life since he had learned that he was a father.

The drive to the small, local market located on the main highway running the length of the island took Andres just a few minutes despite the busy tourist traffic. The parking lot was full of cars so he had to park along the edge of the pavement several hundred feet from the store.

For a moment he hesitated. He was still struggling with the embarrassment of having to use a cane in public. Glancing at the distance he had to cover to reach the market entrance, he finally swallowed his pride and picked up the mortifying symbol of his disability before heading for what he hoped was an air-conditioned store interior.

A burst of cool air washed over him as the automatic door swung open in front of him, and he stepped into the busy establishment that appeared to offer not only a wide selection of fresh, frozen, and canned foods but also fishing gear, boating supplies, beach wear, and souvenirs of the Outer Banks region. He pulled a plastic cart from a row near the entrance and, looping the curved top of the cane over the handle, began to make his way along the aisles crowded with chattering and laughing patrons.

He was not really sure where to begin. It had been a very long time since he had actually prepared food for himself. The nature of his assignments usually required him to give up a regular meal schedule. He often had to settle for a sandwich or a quick cup of coffee, when it was possible, and to skip meals altogether when stopping to eat was impossible. Having the opportunity to shop for and then to prepare a meal was an activity he had stopped many years ago to fulfill professional responsibilities.

He was studying a display of fresh melons when he thought he heard his name. Looking up, he felt a light tug on his arm.

"Andres! I thought that was you. Are you buying groceries too?"

As his gaze met the bright blue eyes of Tanner Bennett, he smiled. "*Mi charro!* What a surprise!"

He noted that the child had changed from the cowboy boots he had been wearing on the porch into clean, white canvas sneakers while still wearing the Stetson hat on his blond head. From beneath the brim, the small boy beamed up at him.

Andres turned to meet Eve's astonished expression as she rounded the corner of the display with her own cart. When her face paled, it emphasized the spray of freckles across the bridge of her nose.

She cleared her throat. "Well, hello."

"Hi, Noo-noo! Hi, Noo-noo!" Andy bounced in her seat in the cart and waved both of her little hands at him.

The unbridled enthusiasm of the two children warmed his heart and eased some of the disappointment he experienced from Eve's unmistakably cool reception of him. He reached out to pat his daughter's curly head. "It must be the day to food shop. This place is packed."

He glanced at the assortment of items in the bottom of the cart behind Andy and then turned his gaze back to Eve. "There are just too many choices for me. I'm having a hard time making any selections at all."

Tanner tapped a honeydew with his knuckles. "You have to thump a melon like this, Mom says, to see if it's ripe. Listen to the sound."

"Does that one sound like it's ready to eat? Should I get it?"

The little boy nodded. "But you should probably get one of each."

Andres stared at the large display of fruit. "There are at least three different kinds of melons."

Tanner nodded again with a solemn expression on his face. "To make sure you get all of the important vitamins you need, you should have all three. Get a green one, an orange one, and a red one. Mom says the more colors you eat, the more vitamins you get."

Andres directed his questioning eyes toward Eve and watched as her cheeks began to blush to an attractive shade of pink. An odd sense of delight stirred in a spot deep inside of him, and he wondered if the strange feeling came from the unexpected meeting of such an enchanting woman in front of the melon stand.

He took a slow, deep breath. "Is that really true, Eve? Food colors matter?"

"Of course it's true." Tanner picked up a cantaloupe and tapped it. "Mom knows all about stuff like that. Too much soda and too much candy are bad for your teeth too."

Andres sighed with a dramatic drop of his shoulders. "Grocery shopping is more complicated than I imagined. Maybe you'd better help me, *mi charro.*"

The little boy's face glowed. "Sure, Andres. Mom and Andy can help too." He thumped another melon. "Hey, I've got an idea. You can come to our house afterward, and Mom can give you a cooking lesson. Then you can stay for dinner."

He looked up at the child's mother, who had remained silent through the whole conversation. "Isn't that a great plan, Mom? Andres needs some help with food, and you know how to cook. You'll teach him, won't you?"

"Oh, Tanner, I'm sure—"

"Please, Mom. Look, he doesn't even know how to choose a melon. We *have* to help him."

Andy held her arms up toward Andres. "Take me out, Noo-noo!"

"It's not Noo-noo, silly." Tanner shook his head. "This is Andres, I mean, your dad. Andres is your father, Andy. Call him *Daddy*."

"Daddy! Daddy! Pick me up."

Tanner looked up at Andres. "She just wants to get out of the cart. She likes to run around loose and get into things."

Andres smiled at the little boy. "So she likes to explore?"

"Yes, and you have to hold on tightly to her. Don't let her go for anything."

Andres turned to Eve. "May I take her?"

A shadow crossed her pretty face, and he thought she might refuse his request. He watched her as she smoothed Andy's curly hair.

"Should you? Your leg—"

He followed her eyes to the spot where they had settled on his cane looped over the handle of his shopping car. "I'm fine, really."

After a moment, she nodded and then stood back as he lifted the bouncing child into his arms. Andy immediately reached for his Saint Isidore medal and twisted the silver chain around her tiny fingers.

"Now, let's see. What else do you like to eat?" Tanner headed down the aisle toward a display of fresh vegetables. "We're having grilled chicken for dinner. Mom'll show you how to cook it so it's nice and juicy. Right, Mom?"

"Now, Tanner, I'm sure Andres has already made other plans."

Andres struggled to hold the active child in his arms. "Actually, I haven't. I just rented the Wetmore place this afternoon and haven't had a chance to think about what to do for dinner."

"The Wetmore place?"

He thought her face could not grow any paler, but her cheeks turned almost white. Her fingers fluttered at the neckline of her loose cotton T-shirt topping a worn denim skirt that brushed her knees.

"I want to spend more time with Andy, and I thought staying nearby would be the best way to accomplish that."

"You're living right next door to us? Really, Andres? Oh, this is just great! Isn't it great, Mom?"

Andres could not read Eve's expression as she turned

toward a large basket of peaches and began to select pieces of fruit to place in her cart, but he was sure she did not seem particularly thrilled with the idea of his sudden move into her neighborhood. He wondered what was wrong. Was she having reservations about his continued involvement in his daughter's life?

Tanner pulled on his mother's arm. "We can eat together all of the time now, Mom. Won't that be fun? You can teach Andres how to grill chicken tonight. Tomorrow you can cook steaks with him and do pork chops the next night." The little boy grinned at Andres. "Mmm, I love Mom's pork chops. She stuffs them with raisins and walnuts and all sorts of good things."

Intercepting Andy's fingers as they attempted to clutch a bunch of red grapes from a nearby bin, Andres lifted his eyebrows in growing interest. "Stuffed pork chops? They sound delicious."

Eve set a hand on the top of her son's hat and tipped her head up to meet Andres' eyes. Her delicate lips curved, and his heart fluttered. Her smile warmed him from head to foot.

"Of course you're welcome to join us for dinner, Andres. We'd be happy to have you as our guest any time."

Tanner grinned again as he slipped a hand into Andres' free one. "You can eat with us, but you'll need some healthy snacks if you get hungry between meals or before you go to bed. Let's find some good things for you to buy."

Pushing the cart, Tanner led Andres down the aisle as

Andy bounced against his hip and reached for items all along the way. Eve, he noticed, trailed a few feet behind them with her own cart and said very little except when Tanner or Andy spoke to her or asked her a question.

As they approached the checkout area, Andres stepped aside to allow Eve to precede him through the line. He tightened his hold on Andy as she stretched out her little arms and struggled to grasp Eve's arm.

"I can take her now, if you'd like."

He nodded and kissed the top of his daughter's curly head before handing her back to the petite, auburn-haired woman. "I guess she wants you."

He watched Eve give Andy a gentle squeeze before placing the child back in the seat in the front of her cart. Anyone watching them would presume that Eve was her mother. Would people seeing the little group buying groceries think that he was the child's father?

"Hey, Andres! I have another great idea!"

"What's that, *mi charro*?" He tapped the brim of the small boy's hat and looked down into bright blue eyes. Tanner's growing fondness for him was obvious in the child's expression, but Andres wondered if he was worthy of such admiration. Could he live up to the expectations a child like Tanner might have for him?

A stab of uneasiness twisted in the pit of his stomach. Was Eve too, worried about her son's developing attachment to him? Was she questioning the wisdom of his decision to rent the house next door to her and to plan to spend more time with her family? Was that the reason she had become so quiet and pensive as they moved through the store?

"Well, can I?"

Andres realized that while his thoughts had preoccupied him, Tanner had been speaking. "Can you what?"

"I mean, may I ride home with you in your car? You live right next to us now. We could talk about fishing or horses or your ranch in Mexico on our way back home."

"New Mexico, and yes, you may ride back with me, as long as it's okay with your mother."

He caught Eve's gaze as she loaded paper bags filled with groceries into the back of her cart. Then she opened a small plastic pouch of raisins for Andy before shaking her head. As she did, strands of loose auburn hair brushed her slender shoulders.

"No, Tanner."

"Oh, please, Mom."

She put another bag of raisins in her son's outstretched hand. "You're still driving that little red sports car, aren't you?" She directed her question to Andres as he paid for his items and collected his bags.

"I understand now that food colors are important to my health, but car colors matter too?"

She narrowed her green eyes at him. "Your sports car doesn't have a backseat."

"No, it doesn't. Do I need one?"

"Tanner is too small to sit in the front, even with a safety belt. Don't you know it's dangerous for young children to ride in the front seat of any car?"

He replaced the cart he had used in the row of empty ones next to the door and then lifted his bags into his arms. Then he reached for his cane.

"I did not know."

"Does that mean I really can't ride with Andres, Mom?"

As Eve moved through the automatic door with her cart, Andres juggled to balance the groceries and cane while trying to conceal his limp. Sharp pains from the constant stopping and starting in the store aisles stabbed at his already aching leg.

He knew he should return home to rest, but he did not look forward to spending the evening alone in a new, unfamiliar place. On the other hand, the idea of sharing another one of Eve's delectable meals with her family in her comfortable home had an undeniable appeal.

"Please, Mom, couldn't we break that silly rule just this once?"

She stopped and touched her son's shoulder. "It's a rule for a reason, Tanner. It was made to keep you safe. I love you, and I don't want anything bad to happen to you."

She smiled. "I know it sounds like I'm being mean, but you and Andres will be able to talk about fishing and horses as soon as he gets to our house."

"Aw, Mom—"

"Your mother is right, *mi charro.*" Balancing the grocery bags and cane, Andres squatted beside the little boy. "It is hard to understand, but she just wants what is best for you. If I want you and Andy to ride with me, then I will have to get a more practical vehicle."

He looked up at Eve. "One with enough room for child safety seats in the back." He tapped the brim of Tanner's hat. "I will meet you at your house in just a few minutes, okay?"

The little boy slumped his shoulders. "All right. I guess it's okay, but I really wanted to ride with you."

Trying to find something to distract the disappointed child, Andres scanned the parking area of the grocery store as he rose to his feet. "Hey, look at that man standing over there by those crepe myrtle bushes. He has a hat that looks like it is just perfect for fishing. Do you know him?"

Andy squealed in the cart as both Eve and her son turned and looked in the direction Andres indicated. The man, whose face was shaded by the large hat he was wearing, spun around and walked away from the parked cars as soon as he appeared to notice that they were watching him.

"We don't know that man, do we, Mom?"

Andres studied Eve as she caught her lower lip between her teeth and furrowed her brow. Something was wrong. Eve Bennett looked worried.

"No, I don't think I recognize him." She smiled, but concern covered her face. "Let's go home."

Chapter Four

After loading Eve's groceries into the back of her sport utility vehicle and helping Tanner, at the child's insistence, to fasten the restraints of his safety seat, Andres headed for his own car. He set his bags in the passenger seat and started the air-conditioning while he watched Eve pull out of the grocery store parking lot. Tanner's hand waved in rapid movements as the little boy pressed his face to the window and grinned.

Andres smiled to himself. Eve's son was a remarkable child. Tanner's immediate acceptance of him was almost overwhelming, but Andres could not deny that he enjoyed spending time with the youngster.

As he followed Eve out onto the main highway that ran the length of Hatteras Island, he acknowledged the realization that, until he had learned he was a father, he had had little interest in children. In fact, he had been rather apathetic toward kids and their endless needs and chatter and immature behavior.

Now, his tiny curly haired daughter's happiness and well-being, as well as that of her older brother, were of prime importance to him. He wanted to keep them safe. Not being able to give Tanner a ride home because he did not have the proper child safety seat had bothered Andres.

The little boy intrigued him. Tanner's assessment of his younger sister was often harsh in its honesty. Although he seemed to be able to understand that Andy was still very young, his impatience with the little girl was almost amusing to Andres.

Those behaviors Andres perceived as intelligent and creative for a two-year-old, such as her competent ability to speak and to reason, Tanner saw as childish and messy. Her calling him *Noo-noo* sounded delightful to Andres while the nickname annoyed her older brother every time she used it.

And the boy's mother. Andres could not help but appreciate the way Eve managed her parenting role with unquestionable proficiency and good nature. She had certainly impressed him. On the other hand, she did not seem to be very pleased with either his decision to move into the house next door or his desire to spend more time with Andy and her family. He was quite sure she had invited him to dinner that evening only because Tanner had insisted. Eve's impeccable manners dictated that she extend the invitation because it would appear impolite if she did not.

Well, he would have to work on improving that situation. He was not sure why, but it was important to him that he make a good impression on the pretty, young woman. If he had to do it, he would use all of the captivating charm he could muster to convince her that he was not the naïve, self-centered, and reckless individual she had judged him to be.

The woman was tough. He supposed that she had to be to raise, with such obvious commitment and care, two small children all on her own. He liked her. He admired her integrity, her determination, and her common sense. He even liked her directness. Eve Bennett was not afraid to express her opinions.

Andres sighed. She was, in his mind, nearly perfect. She was attractive in a natural, unsophisticated sort of way. She displayed a kind of grace, an unassuming beauty, and a delightful sense of humor when she was not concentrating on a stiff adherence to rules and propriety.

Despite Eve's many positive attributes, Andres could never describe her as glamorous or worldly. She was nothing like Cheryl, who had always worn the latest fashions and had spent hours a week with her hairdresser, manicurist, and personal fitness trainer.

While his ex-wife had been tall and thin and almost

obsessive about weight, Eve was petite with appealing feminine curves. In fact, she had very nice curves in all of the right places.

Curves? In an instant, a caution light flashed in Andres' mind, and he almost missed the right turn onto the street leading to Eve's quiet, residential waterfront neighborhood. What was he doing thinking about Eve and her curves in that way?

Of course, he could not possibly be attracted to the young woman who was the guardian of his daughter. Eve Bennett was a lovely, caring woman who worked hard and spent much time denying her own feelings and needs while she focused almost all of her attention on taking care of the needs of others.

Yes, she was attractive. He would allow himself to admit that fact. Her slender neck and smooth shoulders brushed by thick wavy strands of auburn hair were enticing. Her toned legs and pretty ankles were also interesting.

Suddenly, he caught himself again. What was he thinking? How could he allow himself such mental wonderings about a woman he hardly knew?

Swallowing, he slowed his own vehicle as Eve signaled and then pulled into her driveway. With a racing heart, Andres waved again to Tanner and drove past the sport utility vehicle to the house he had rented next door.

"Come right up, Andres." Tanner, in cowboy attire, leaned over the edge of the porch and waved as he gave

Andres the broadest welcoming smile he had ever seen in his life.

Grasping the railing for support, he ascended the single flight of stairs and rounded the house to the well-shaded back portion of the porch facing the picturesque inlet of Pamlico Sound. Andy's curls bounced around her tiny face as she bounded toward him. He noted that a gate across the steps leading to the water was fastened to keep the child safe despite her impulsive, continual, and determined explorations.

As he scooped the little girl into his arms, Eve gave him a wave from her seat on the bench attached to the perimeter of the porch. She offered him a glass of fruit juice from the pitcher on a nearby table. Andres saw the faint lines of fatigue on her forehead when she brushed damp bangs away from her drawn face.

"We're taking a little rest before dinner." Tanner plopped down on the bench beside his mother. "We worked really hard before we went grocery shopping today."

Balancing Andy in one arm, Andres accepted the juice from Eve and took a long drink of the sweet, pulpy liquid. "And what kind of work did you do today, *mi charro*?"

"We washed all of the windows, inside and out. Mom had to climb up on the step ladder, but I made sure she didn't fall."

"Good for you." He turned to study the wooden exterior of the cottage. "That's a lot of windows."

"Twenty-eight. I counted them as we washed. Andy helped too, with her own paper towels." Holding his cowboy hat, Tanner tilted his head to one side and looked at the little girl Andres held in his arm. "Well, maybe she didn't help all that much. Mostly she just played with her toys and sang us songs."

"Songs?"

"You know, baby songs, like 'Old MacDonald Had a Farm' and 'Mary Had a Little Lamb.' Hey, Andres, do you play the guitar?"

"Play blocks, Noo-noo."

Andres set Andy on the porch and squatted to begin piling plastic blocks in a rectangular formation. "I'm afraid I don't play any instrument, Tanner. Do you?"

The little boy shook his head. "No, but maybe we could learn. Together, I mean. Lots of good cowboy songs need guitar music, don't you think?"

"I'm sure you're right. That sounds like a good goal for us, *mi charro*. What other work did you and your mother do today?"

"We changed all of the beds and did the laundry."

Andres whistled and looked at Eve, who was leaning down to help Andy stack blocks into a wobbling tower. He tried to ignore the way his heart began to race as he watched her loose auburn hair brush her shoulders and fall over her creamy cheeks.

"You seem to have accomplished quite a lot today."

Handing him a block, Tanner shook his head. "Not everything. We have to finish water-sealing the porch.

We did all of the steps and the sides this morning, but we still have to do this part right here in the back."

Eve reached out and removed Tanner's hat from his hand. Combing her fingers through the child's matted blond hair, she smiled. "We'll do that tomorrow, I guess. We have to have dinner, and you and Andy each need to soak in the tub tonight to wash off all that dirt and grime you've accumulated today."

Andres met her pretty yet tired green eyes. "You look like you could use a nice, warm, relaxing hour in a bubble bath too."

"Because Mom's kind of dirty, just like we are?"

Still holding Eve's gaze, Andres chuckled. "No, because I think she deserves a little fun time just for herself once in a while."

She smiled as she handed Andy a small plastic cup of juice. "I don't know too many single mothers with young children who get the opportunity for such luxuries very often."

"Uh-oh, Mommy."

Eve reached out to catch the cup as it slipped from Andy's hands but did not reach the little girl before she spilled orange juice all the way down the front of her shirt. "Well, sweetie, it looks like you need to get cleaned up right now."

Lifting the grinning child into her arms, Eve turned to Andres. "It's too hard to clean up this sticky mess with a washcloth, so I'll just give her a quick bath before I start dinner."

"What can we do while we wait, Mom?"

Eve smiled. "Just sit and relax. Andy and I will be done in just a few minutes."

Andres reached out to finger a curl on his daughter's shoulder, but she bounced against Eve's hip and pulled away from his hand. "No, Noo-noo. I want Mommy."

Andres could not tell if Eve appeared relieved or not, but the young woman touched Andy's chin with her fingertips. "Blow a kiss to your daddy now, and later, maybe he'll read you a storybook."

The child gave her curly head a firm shake. "I want Mommy! I want Mommy!"

Eve's green eyes met Andres' gaze. "She's a little tired now. She likes you, but she's still a little shy. Be patient."

Nodding, Andres watched Eve and Andy enter the house through the sliding glass doors. Setting a hand on Tanner's shoulder, he sighed. "Well, *mi charro*, it looks like we have some work to do. We have to water-seal this part of the porch. Do you know where your mother keeps the paintbrushes?"

"What a great idea! Do you really mean that I can help you?" The boy's blue eyes grew wide. "Really?"

Andres nodded. "If we want to get done before Andy finishes her bath, we'd better hurry."

Tanner beamed. "I know where everything is, but first we'll have to move the table and Andy's blocks."

"Right. You know more about taking care of this

house than I do. Just tell me what you need, boss, and I'll do it."

When Eve emerged from the bathroom, her sleeveless cotton blouse was damp with splashes from Andy's bathwater. The activity had taken much longer than usual because first Andy had insisted on playing with her rubber toys, and then she had been uncooperative about getting her hair washed. As a result, Eve felt tired and hungry and in no mood to make polite conversation or to try to entertain the dark, Latin man who was now living, at least temporarily, right next door to her.

Andy, happy once again and in a clean, dry sundress with a ruffled hem that fell just below her little knees, ran ahead of her into the living room and plopped down on the floor. Eve left the child leafing through a storybook as she headed through the dining room to prepare dinner.

Entering the galley kitchen, she was surprised to find Andres and her son already there. From his seat on top of the counter near the sink, Tanner smiled at her.

"Hi, Mom. We were just getting ready to start cooking." He held up his hands and turned them from palm to back several times. "We scrubbed up and everything. What should we do first?"

Eve brushed her bangs off her forehead. "Get down off the counter before you fall."

"I'm not going to fall."

"Tanner."

Her son sent a hopeful glance to Andres, who shrugged his broad shoulders but remained silent. With a shrug of his own small shoulders, Tanner conceded to her demand. "All right. I'll get down, but I know I wasn't going to fall."

He slid onto a chair next to the counter and kneeled on the seat. "Okay, Andres and I are ready. Tell us what you want us to do."

Eve sighed. She would have preferred to be alone in the kitchen. It would be so much easier to go ahead and do what she needed to do without two eager assistants hovering nearby and waiting for her instructions.

"What are we having with the chicken, Mom?"

"Rice and salad and frozen yogurt with fresh fruit for dessert."

"Mmm. It sounds delicious. I'm really hungry."

She raised her gaze and found Andres' deep brown eyes watching her. An unexpected rush of warmth flooded her body and made her knees weak. She cleared her throat.

"Tanner, why don't you get the baby spinach and carrots from the refrigerator and start washing them while I put the rice on and then help Andres make the chicken glaze?"

"Good idea." Her son jumped off the chair. "May I chop the walnuts if I'm very, *very* careful?"

She filled a saucepan with water and set it on the stove. "Maybe. Wash the vegetables first."

Handing Andres a stick of butter and a bowl, she glanced into the living room at Andy who was still browsing at the collection of storybooks on the floor within her reach. "Take off the wrapper and melt this in the microwave. It'll take about twenty seconds."

As the tall, dark man nodded and proceeded to follow her directions, her initial nervousness about having him in the kitchen began to subside. Maybe it would not be so bad preparing a meal with Andres Nunez as long as he did not insist that she engage in any conversation beyond that needed to get dinner on the table.

When the time came to grill the chicken breasts, Andres offered to watch them on the barbecue on the porch just outside one of the kitchen doors. While he and Tanner turned the poultry—at frequent intervals according to her directions—to keep the pieces from burning, and then coated them with glaze as they finished cooking, Eve mixed the dressing for the salad and set the table.

They ate the meal as Tanner chatted about fishing and horses while Andy offered her comments about the food or something she found amusing or interesting in her own little two-year-old world. Andres helped Tanner with dressing for his salad and cut Andy's chicken into small pieces.

Eve sometimes caught Andres looking at her when he was not busy helping the children. The unsolicited attention caused a heated blush to rise on her cheeks. With effort, she pulled away from his gaze and forced her concentration back to her children.

When they finished dinner, she began to clear the table. "Tanner, why don't you and Andy take Andres outdoors now that it's cooler? I'm sure Andy will dig in her sandbox if you and Andres want to play ball."

Andres touched her arm with his hand. "Please, let me help clean up first." His charming smile made her heart pound. "Part of learning to prepare a meal is cleaning up afterward, right, *mi charro*?"

He winked at Tanner, and Eve could not help but smile as the child winked back. Although he had always been friendly and extroverted, her son had never bonded so quickly with anyone as he had with Andres Nunez. She was not sure she was comfortable with that fact.

"Right, Andres. Come on. I'll show you how to load the dishwasher, and then we can practice pitching baseball in the backyard. I've been working on my fastball."

While Tanner instructed Andres on arranging dirty plates and glasses in the racks and the silverware in the basket of the dishwasher, Eve cleaned Andy's hands and face and then put on a DVD of children's songs to play in the living room. Returning to the kitchen, she ran water in the dishpan and added liquid soap so she could wash the pans and lids they had used to prepare dinner.

Tanner poured cleaning powder into the compartment in the open door of the dishwasher and then closed it. With a smile of triumph, he pushed the power button and started the machine's cleaning process.

"I'll go get the baseball and mitts. I have an extra glove for you. It belongs to Grandpa, but he won't mind if you use it."

Eve reached for the dishtowel, but Andres had already found it and was wiping a pot she had rinsed and set in the dish drainer. He met her eyes with the now familiar, if still unsettling, mysterious magnetic hold.

"Dinner was excellent."

She felt her cheeks heat as they blushed from his simple compliment. "It was an easy meal. Nothing fancy."

"You prepare meals like that all the time?"

She nodded. "Meat. Rice. Salad. That's a basic Bennett dinner."

He lifted a lid with long, tanned fingers and began to wipe it. "It may have started out as basic, but all the little extras you added made the meal superb."

He dried another pan. "You'll have to write down your recipes for the chicken glaze and salad dressing. I'll never be able to remember all of the ingredients."

She shook her head. "I'm afraid I don't use recipes most of the time. I usually just guess at amounts and, sometimes, even ingredients, depending on what I have available at the time."

He lifted his brows above deep brown eyes that looked at her with intense scrutiny. For what was he searching? Her legs felt unsteady as his gaze unnerved her. She raised a hand to the collar of her blouse and fingered the thin cotton fabric.

"Tell me why you bother."

She swallowed. "Bother with what?"

"Grating the orange peel and melting the butter and honey into a delectable glaze for grilled chicken or chopping dates and walnuts and shredding carrots to make a spinach salad with a tasty homemade lemon raspberry vinaigrette dressing? Wouldn't Tanner and Andy eat the food you prepare without all of the fuss?"

She smiled as his serious mouth widened into a lopsided grin. At that moment, she thought Andres Nunez was the most intriguing man she had ever met.

"Yes, they probably would. Both children have good appetites and are not picky at all. I suppose I bother with the little extras because I would like them to grow up knowing there are always choices in life, even when it comes to what they eat. I want Tanner and Andy to try a variety of foods and learn to decide for themselves what they like and don't like as they get older."

He nodded, and a strand of dark hair fell across his forehead. He picked up the last rinsed lid. "Ah, a sound belief, but do the recipients of your diligence appreciate your efforts?"

Eve smiled. "Probably not, but I've found that most of the actions parents make as caregivers, except ones to fulfill immediate basic needs of our children, do not show results right away. We all must wait and see the kind of children we have raised when they have finally grown up into adults and have begun to make their own decisions. Only then are we able to determine if we accomplished what we set out to do."

When he brushed aside the rogue strand of hair, Eve's breath caught in her throat. Why did she have such an intense reaction to his nearness?

"And the accomplishment would be what?"

"To have raised healthy, happy children into unselfish and responsible men and women."

His brown eyes held her gaze again. "How do you manage to stay cheerful and caring when you are faced with the burden of such high aspirations?"

She shrugged and ignored the racing of her heart. "I suppose I manage by considering parenthood not as a burden but as a challenge and a blessing."

"Here's your mitt, Andres. Let's go play some baseball."

Tanner's enthusiastic words brought their philosophical conversation to an end. Eve inhaled a long, deep breath as she watched Andres fold the damp dish towel and set it on the counter before striding through the dining room to squat next to his little daughter, still engrossed in the children's musical DVD on television.

"*Mi niñita*, Rosita. Are you coming outside to watch us play ball?"

Tanner tugged on his arm. "Why do you call her *mi niñita*, Andres?"

"*Mi niñita* means 'my little one'."

"*Mi niñita* and *mi charro*. We both have new names. What about Mom? Do you have a special name for her?"

Andres rose to his full height and smiled down at the

little boy. Eve is *Eva* in Spanish. We could call her *Evita*, or little Eva."

"She's not little. She's a mom." Tanner studied her as she approached the group in the living room. "But I guess you're right. When she stands next to you, Mom's really small."

Andres' brown eyes caught hers in a steady gaze. "She may be small in size, but she has an amazingly big heart."

Tanner grinned. "How do you know how big her heart is? You can't even see it. Come on. Let's go play."

"Andy, honey." Eve held out her hand to the little girl. "Let's go watch the guys toss the baseball for a while."

After turning off the DVD player and television, she scooped the child into her arms. As she opened the sliding door leading to the back porch, Tanner stopped her.

"Not that way, Mom. We have to go out the side door."

"What's wrong with this one?"

"The water seal on the porch might not be dry yet."

"We didn't get to it, Tanner. Don't you remember?"

Her son grinned at her. "Andres and I did it while you were giving Andy her bath. We even cleaned up the brushes and put everything away in the storage cabinet."

"You did?" Eve did not try to hide her astonishment as she lifted her eyes to receive confirmation from the tall, handsome man pounding his fist into the worn leather baseball mitt on his hand.

"Yes, ma'am." Andres' grin was as wide as Tanner's

as he set his ungloved hand on her son's shoulder and met her gaze. "This young man of yours is a very hard worker."

She swallowed as an uncomfortable mixture of appreciation and apprehension flooded through her. While she experienced relief that the task of water-sealing the back porch was complete, she did not want to be indebted to Andres. She did not want to let herself get used to his presence.

"You didn't have to do that, Andres."

His grin broadened. "We wanted to help out, didn't we, *mi charro*? We were happy to do it."

From her seat at the picnic table on the side porch of her parents' beach cottage, Eve had a full view of the shaded back and side yards. She could also see the Wetmore house to her left and the quiet street where they resided. She divided her attention between watching the antics of Tanner and Andres' baseball practice, in which the two seemed to do more chasing than catching and pitching, and making sure Andy stayed in her round plastic sandbox and away from the recently sealed back porch and the steps leading down to the ground.

After over an hour of playing ball, Tanner and Andres moved on to tag and then dodgeball with a large rubber ball. Eve noticed that although Andres gave his full concentration to her son when he was with him, he frequently excused himself from their mutual activities to climb the steps and to sit with Andy in her sandbox. He took a few minutes every time to speak with her and to fill a pail or dig a hole or drive a toy dump truck around the mounds of sand.

If she were honest with herself, she would have to admit that Andres appeared to be making a genuine effort to become acquainted with his daughter without undue disruption of the child's life. On the other hand, Eve realized that her family would probably never be the same again. She was not sure she was prepared to face that change quite yet.

With a sigh, Eve lifted a sleepy Andy onto her lap and allowed her eyes to roam from the dock, where Tanner was busy explaining to Andres the differences between surf fishing and fishing in the sound, to the silent Wetmore house. She wondered how long Andres would be staying there. As of yet, he had not explained what exactly had motivated him to rent the place next door to her, and she had not figured out a polite way to ask him about his intentions.

Unidentified movement to her far left caught her attention, and she pulled her gaze from the four-story residence to the street. She saw a compact car parked across from her driveway. From it emerged a figure that appeared vaguely familiar to her. Had the car broken down right there on the street?

Although the individual stood too far away for her to determine if the person was a man or a woman, Eve could see that whoever was standing beside the car was wearing some kind of large head covering and seemed to be looking in the direction of her parents' cottage. She wondered if someone needed help.

As she studied the individual on the roadside, recollection came to her in an instant. The man standing there was the same man at the grocery store earlier that afternoon. He was the one who had been wearing the canvas hat and baggy cargo pants. *What is he doing in front of our house?*

She turned to call to Andres and Tanner on the dock and was surprised to find her tall, dark guest ascending the nearest steps. She hoped she would be able to hide how upset she felt at the moment.

"Is she asleep?" He glanced down at the drowsy child in her arms.

"Not yet." Eve tightened her hold on Andy and gave the man across the street another nervous glance.

She jumped as Andres touched her shoulder. He stared down at her with a surprised expression on his handsome face. "Eve? What is it? What's wrong?"

Her attempt to make her tone natural was futile. Her voice trembled with rising fear. "That man by the car across the street. I think he's watching us."

He followed her gaze. "What man?"

"Over there. Next to that small parked car."

"How long?"

She felt herself shake in spite of her resolve to remain

calm. Rising to her feet, she tried to get a better look at the stranger with the canvas hat. "What do you mean?" Her voice was a breathless whisper.

Andres grasped her arm. "Do you know how long he's been standing there?"

"No, I just noticed him."

"Wait here." His command was firm as he touched Andy's curly head. "And keep the kids here with you too."

With long, hurried strides, he crossed the porch and rushed down the front steps toward the street. Eve held her breath and rocked her daughter in her arms as she watched Andres' tall figure move along the length of the driveway.

"Hey, Mom. Where'd Andres go?"

Tanner's question drew her eyes to the steps leading to the side yard where her son was hopping up and down in obvious impatience. "Where is he? Did he have to go get a drink? I'm getting really thirsty too."

"That's a good idea, Tanner." She forced a smile. "Come on into the house, and we'll all have some lemonade."

Tanner and Andy were sitting by the dining room table when Andres returned a few minutes later. The little boy ran to his side. "Where've you been? Come and have a cold drink with us."

Eve's hands were still shaking as she poured Andres a glass of lemonade. Although she was anxious to discover the identity of the stranger, she did not want to speak in front of Tanner and was grateful that Andres seemed to understand.

While Tanner took his bath, Andres read Andy a short bedtime story and helped Eve tuck the little girl into bed. At Tanner's insistence, Andres then read a chapter to him from the action adventure story Eve had started a few nights ago with him, and then said good night.

After closing her son's bedroom door, she led Andres into the living room and offered him a seat. "Would you like some coffee or tea?" She was anxious to hear what he had to say about the stranger, but she did not want to seem impolite.

"No, thank you."

Sitting in a chair near him, she could contain her questions no longer. "What did you find out? What did that man want?"

She watched Andres lower himself with care onto the couch. Was his leg bothering him again? He had not used his cane since they had met him in the grocery store earlier that afternoon.

"I'm not sure, Eve."

"What do you mean? Wouldn't he tell you?"

Andres sighed. "When I got across the street, he had already driven off. He was in such a hurry that I didn't even have a chance to get his license number."

"License number?" She chewed her lower lip. "Do

you think it's that serious? I mean, what do you think he was doing lurking around here?"

Andres looked thoughtful for a moment. "He definitely appeared to be watching this house. Are you sure you don't recognize him?"

"Me? No, not at all."

"You have no idea why someone would be watching you?"

She felt sudden indignation rise within her. All of the frustration she was experiencing over his own sudden appearance in her life tested her patience.

"What about you? Couldn't he be watching you?" With nervous fingers, she played with the collar of her blouse. "I mean, he seemed to appear in the neighborhood after you decided to move into the Wetmore place. He could be spying on you for some reason, couldn't he?"

His chuckle irritated her. "Spying? You may be overreacting just a little, Eve. What possible reason would someone have to be watching me?"

"I don't know." She heard her voice increase in pitch as her agitation heightened. She rose to her feet. "Your work. You talk about kidnappings and political uprisings and attacking insurgents. Your life is not exactly tranquil, Andres."

He stared at her. "I can see that you're very upset about this unidentified man, Eve." He reached out to touch her arm. "You've had a long, hard day. Why don't you sit down and relax."

She pushed away his hand. "No, I don't want to relax, and how I feel has nothing to do with what kind of day I've had. I'm concerned that my family and I are being put in a position of potential danger because of your being here."

"I honestly don't believe that's the case. Do you think I would purposely place my own child, or Tanner and you, for that matter, in a possibly harmful situation?"

"No, not on purpose." She chewed her lower lip for a moment. "But you lead such a different life, Andres, full of recklessness and excitement. I wonder if you can even recognize risky or hazardous circumstances."

He shook his head as he rose from his seat. "We're not getting anywhere arguing about who is the more cautious individual. In addition, I think we may be jumping to conclusions about the man in the canvas hat."

He sighed. "Let's call a truce for the night and continue this discussion when we have more information about the mysterious stranger. I'm fairly sure his car had Virginia plates. I'll call the local police tonight, give them a general description of the man, and ask them to keep a lookout for him. In the meantime, I think we should all be especially alert to any individuals acting or appearing to have undue interest in the children or even in one of us."

Eve inhaled a long, steady breath that failed to calm her nerves. "Do you really think this is serious enough to get the police involved?"

Holding her eyes in his gaze, he set his hands on her

shoulders. This time she did not push him away from her. In fact, she found herself acknowledging, with grudging reluctance, that she welcomed his serene presence and decisive actions. For the first time in many years, she allowed herself to wonder about the idea of having a man in her life, someone with whom to share dreams and accomplishments and worries. She considered what it would be like to rely on someone else, occasionally, for emotional support, rather than living a fulfilling, yet often isolated and lonely, existence as a single parent.

"I don't know how serious this is, Eve, but your safety and peace of mind, as well as the safety of the children, are the immediate issues here. I think we should take as many precautions as we can to protect you. Are all of the cottage windows locked?"

"Yes, I think so." She thought for a moment. "Maybe not all of them. I had to release most of the locks to wash the inside and outside panes today."

He nodded. "I'll check them all before I head back to the Wetmore place." He gave her shoulders a gentle squeeze. "Although the guy with the hat doesn't seem to want to get too close, I think it's a good idea for you to lock the doors as soon as you, Tanner, and Andy are inside. How many entrances are there?"

She chewed her lower lip once again. "All of the sliding doors and the wooden one on the front porch. There's one in the kids' bathroom that leads down below the house to the storage area that I keep locked all of the time. I usually check them before I go to bed."

He smiled. "Just for now, until we figure out what this guy is doing, why don't you keep every door locked, even during the day?"

She gave him a slow, hesitant nod. "I don't like this, Andres."

The warmth of his touch on her skin and the gentle squeeze of his hands on her shoulders sent waves of comfort through her. She inhaled another deep breath and chewed her bottom lip. What did the man with the canvas hat want? Why had he been watching the cottage?

"I'm sure we'll get this figured out soon. I have to go back to Washington for a therapy appointment tomorrow, but I'll be back by evening. I'll leave my mobile phone number with you. I always carry it. Please don't hesitate to call."

He released his hold on her shoulders. "I'll ask the police to keep a close eye on this street and your house tomorrow. That should relieve your concern a little, okay?"

"I guess."

"I know you're tough, Eve Bennett. Tanner tells me that all of the time."

The mention of her son made her smile in spite of her anxious mood. "Sometimes he tends to exaggerate."

Andres shook his head, and she watched a strand of dark hair sweep onto his tanned forehead. "I don't think so. Not about something like this." He smiled. "We'll get this all straightened out, I promise; and if I *am* the object of that guy's disturbing presence, I will personally make sure he never bothers you again."

"Thank you."

"And thank you for inviting me to share the evening with your family. Dinner was delicious, and the company was wonderful, even if the evening is ending on such a distressing note."

Chapter Five

"Tanner, this is the third time I've asked you to pick up your toys in here."

Eve brushed back bangs from her forehead and met the widening blue eyes of her son as she stood near where he sat on the living room floor strewn with hundreds of plastic nuts, bolts, and rods of his erector set. "You know you're not suppose to have all of those small parts out where Andy can reach them, and I've been waiting to vacuum this room for over twenty minutes."

"Andy's in her chair by the table. You said I could play with tiny pieces if she was in her chair or sleeping."

"Well, pick them up now. I need to clean this room."

Tanner shook his head. "You sure are grumpy this morning, Mom." He tipped his blond head and studied her. "You look tired too. Didn't you sleep well?"

Her son's observations astonished her. While it was true that she has not slept for the past two nights, she had hoped that she had not been so transparent that even her seven-year-old son could see how miserable she felt.

A knock on the front porch door interrupted her thoughts, and Tanner rushed past her into the kitchen. "It's Andres, Mom. I knew he'd come today. He promised, and he always keeps his promises."

Eve's heart somersaulted, and she swallowed. She could not figure out why just the mention of Andres Nunez's name made her body react in unusual ways.

"Hey, the door's locked. We never lock this door during the day."

She reached around her son's small shoulder and twisted the latch to release the lock. Her breath caught in her throat as she looked up into the smiling, tanned face of Andy's father.

Andres!" Tanner greeted the visitor by flinging his arms around the tall man's legs and laughing in delight. "We're so glad you're here."

"Buenos dias, mi charro." Andres scooped the little boy into his arms and hugged him. "What a wonderful welcome."

His brown eyes moved from her son to capture Eve's gaze. "Good morning, Eve."

"Noo-noo! Noo-noo! Hi, Noo-noo!"

Eve turned to see Andy bouncing in her high chair, waving her arms, and grinning at her father. As Eve hurried to release the child from the confining seat,

Tanner scrambled out of Andres's arms and rushed past her.

"Don't let her get down yet, Mom. My erector set pieces. Remember?"

"Hi, Noo-noo."

Andy strained against Eve's hold as she reached for Andres. "I blow you kiss, Noo-noo."

"Don't let her go, Andres."

With raised eyebrows, Andres lifted his daughter from Eve's arms and kissed the top of her curly head. "Why not, *mi charro*? What are you building?"

Tanner wrinkled his nose as he looked at his play area on the floor. "I'm not. I have to clean up. Mom's been a little cranky this morning."

Andres was still holding Eve's gaze as he set Andy on his broad shoulders. Bending his knees, he bobbed her up and down while the little girl squealed with pleasure. "She has? What's making her cranky?"

Tanner shrugged. "I don't know. She didn't sleep well, I guess. Maybe she had nightmares."

Andres' expression of concern and intense visual scrutiny made Eve uncomfortable. She tried to pull her eyes away from him, but he held her with his despite the fact that a two-year-old was twisting his ears and dragging her fingers through his hair. Soon her little fingers found the silver chain around his neck.

"Did something keep you awake during the night, Eve?"

She shook her head. "No, nothing in particular."

He untangled the chain from Andy's fingers. "Are you sure?"

She forced a smile. "I'm sure."

"There. All done, Mom." Tanner hurried back to them. "Let's go play in the yard."

To Eve's relief, Andres finally turned his attention to her son. "What are we going to play?"

"I saw a big frog out there yesterday. I want to see if I can find it again. Or maybe it was a toad. Do you know if toads can jump as far as frogs, Andres?"

"I don't know, *mi charro.* I suppose we'll have to look that information up or do some experimenting to find the answer."

The little boy caught his hand as they headed toward the closest sliding door. "Experimenting? Do you mean with frogs and toads?"

"Unless you can come up with a better way to figure out which jumps farther."

Andres slid the door closed, and Eve missed the rest of the conversation. Exhaling a steady sigh, she rushed to a nearby storage closet and pulled out the vacuum cleaner.

Andres Nunez may be a complete disruption in her life, but he was someone she could trust as a dependable babysitter. She could think of no reason why she should not benefit from that fact. Both Tanner and Andy liked him, and he was available and willing to help. Why should she not use the situation to its full advantage?

Still trying to convince herself that it was not against

her better judgment to rely on Andres to watch her children while she accomplished a few tasks around the house, Eve continued with her usual morning chores. She was folding laundry on Tanner's bed sometime later when she heard him return to the house and enter the kitchen with her children.

She dropped a pile of socks in a bureau drawer and set the empty basket in one corner of the room before taking a last sweeping look around the room with its nautical motif to make sure everything was in order, at least for the moment. A need for neatness of his surroundings was not, she admitted, one of Tanner's stronger assets.

Three grinning faces greeted her from their seats at the table as she rounded the corner of the living room and entered the dining area. Each had a glass of ice water in front of him while it appeared that Andres was getting ready to read from one of Andy's picture books.

"Hi, Mom. We're taking a break. It's hot out there today."

As Eve approached the table to grasp Andy's outstretched hand, her feet came in contact with two objects set side by side on the floor. She stumbled to keep her balance, and her surprised gaze fell on the contents of two red plastic pails. One had a brown, lumpy-skinned amphibian on a bed of grass, and the other, a green spotted one in a few inches of water.

"What are those things doing in my kitchen?" Recovering from her astonishment, she set her hands on her hips.

"They're for our experiment, Mom. One toad and one frog."

"*Mi charro,* I thought I told you to set those buckets outside on the porch when we came in."

"I was afraid they'd hop away."

"They can't stay in the kitchen, Tanner."

"I'll take them in the bathroom then."

"Absolutely not."

The child's blue eyes were full of hope. "My bedroom?"

"Tanner Edwin Bennett. Take those creatures out of this house at once. And where did all of this grass come from? It's covering the kitchen floor. Look at your shoes!"

Both Andres and Tanner gave her sheepish looks that almost made her smile. She caught her lower lip between her teeth and narrowed her eyes at them.

"Sorry, Mom. I guess we dragged it in without noticing. It's all from when you mowed the lawn yesterday."

"So, if I hadn't mowed, this mess wouldn't be here in the house right now?" She tried to follow the logic of a seven-year-old but directed her gaze at the dark, handsome man who appeared amused by the entire situation.

She sighed. "You do realize, don't you, that you are both making more work for me?"

"Not on purpose, Mom." Tanner put his hand to his mouth and then, lowering his voice, leaned toward Andres. "See, I told you she was cranky today."

Andres winked at her son as though the two shared

some profound secret of life. "Maybe your mother just needs a little break. She's been working very hard lately. Taking a day to relax might make her feel better."

Tanner shook his head. "Mom said there are no breaks until all of the work around here gets done."

"Oh?" Andres met and held her eyes. "And what work could be so important that it keeps your mother from having a little fun?"

Annoyed by the man's teasing tone, Eve inhaled a deep breath. "Tanner knows that even though this is summer vacation, we still have chores to do. Today, for instance, we have to rake and weed the flowerbeds and trim all of the bushes in the yard. After that, we'll put down fresh mulch."

Her son gave his head a vigorous nod. "Grandpa likes the yard to look nice so we help him every year."

"That sounds like quite a big job, *mi charro*."

Tanner nodded again. "It is. Usually Grandpa's in charge, and Mom and Grandma and I just do whatever he says, but this year Mom and I are doing this work ourselves. Grandpa will be so surprised when he gets here."

The child took a drink from his water glass. "You can help us too, Andres."

Eve watched the handsome man smile and nod. "I would be happy to do what I can. What about Andy?"

"She's too little to help. Sometimes she gets mixed up and pulls the flowers instead of the weeds so it's better if she just plays and follows us around while we work."

Despite Eve's initial annoyance at Andres' inability

to notice or to understand the importance of performing necessary household chores, she felt her aggravation wane to a tentative respect for his diligence and good-natured attitude as they worked. He raked and trimmed and weeded. He also hauled the wheelbarrow loaded with branches and weeds to the side of the street for trash pickup and chased Andy around the yard when the two-year-old decided that she needed more attention than she was receiving by playing alone on the nearby grass.

"Wow! Things are really looking nice around here." Tanner clapped his hands and grinned as he stood in the center of the side yard. "We did a great job!"

Eve removed her gardening gloves and smiled at her son. "Grandpa would be proud of you."

"Of *us*, Mom. All of us. Hey, Andres, you're going to like Grandpa. He doesn't ride horses, but he's good at baseball, and he catches really big fish."

Eve watched the tall man smile down at her son while he struggled to keep a firm hold on Andy who bounced up and down with ceaseless energy in his arms. Her heart warmed at the sight of him with the two children.

"I look forward to meeting him, *mi charro*, and your grandmother too. Will they be coming soon?"

"Not yet. Aunt Jeanne still hasn't had her baby. Grandma called last night before I went to bed. She said that the baby might wait one or two more weeks yet."

Eve took a step closer to Tanner. "Andres may not be able to stay until then. He doesn't have a long break from his job like you and I have from school."

Her son's shoulders slumped, and disappointment filled his blue eyes. "I wish you could stay all summer." He tipped his blond head to look up at the man towering over him. "Couldn't you tell your boss you need more time with us?"

"It doesn't work that way, *mi charro.*" Andres reached out and tousled the little boy's hair. "But I promise we'll spend as much time together as we can. We're partners, right?"

"Yup, partners." His eyes brightened. "We're friends, Andres. And friends spend lots of time together. You like spending time with us, don't you?"

He nodded as he used gentle movements to pull Andy's fingers from their determined grip on the chain around his neck. "I do, Tanner. Very much."

Eve was sure Andres' response was genuine. She knew he seemed to enjoy spending time with Tanner and Andy, but did he have the sense of commitment he needed to be a real father to Andy, not to mention the energy and time her son was already expecting of him? The whole situation was becoming so complicated.

With a sigh, she forced a smile. "Let's go have some lunch, and then we'll head over to the hardware store in town to get the mulch we need to finish the work around the yard."

"Lunch? Great! What are we having?"

Andy reached for Eve. "Mommy! I want Mommy."

Andres handed the squirming child to her. "Would you like me to go out and get something already prepared?"

She shook her head. "Thank you, but that's not necessary. Everything is ready. We're having tuna salad on lettuce and vanilla yogurt with fresh berries."

"Come on, Mom. Let's go in. I'm hungry."

While Andres hurried next door to change his clothes, Eve and the children washed up and changed their own clothes. When Andres returned, they sat down and enjoyed the simple cold lunch that Eve had prepared earlier that day.

After they had finished eating, Tanner and Andres helped Eve clean up the kitchen and load the dishwasher. They then headed outdoors once again.

"Let's take my vehicle today."

Eve turned to look at Andres, who was following her down the steps. With patience, she inhaled a slow breath and smiled at him as though she would at one of the children if Tanner or Andy persisted on arguing about some unreasonable or inappropriate position.

"I've already explained that—"

His broad smile reached all the way up to his sparkling, mischievous brown eyes as he held up his hand to stop her from continuing. "I know. The sports car was unsuitable to transport children safely so I exchanged it for a more acceptable means of transportation."

"Hey, look, Mom. Andres has a new car." With his cowboy hat shading his blue eyes, Tanner pointed across the lawn to the Wetmore driveway where Eve saw a large silver sport utility vehicle parked. "It's almost as big and fancy as Grandpa's. Does it have a DVD player so kids can watch movies while they ride in it?"

Andres nodded. "And it also has a car seat for a two-year-old girl and a booster seat for a seven-year-old boy." He grinned at Eve. "I had to have a sales clerk at the department store help me select the right models. There were too many colors and styles and features for me to choose from all on my own. How do parents do it?"

She felt her eyes widen in astonishment. Warmth washed over her as she imagined Andres, alone and confused, taking the time to search long store aisles for proper car restraints for Tanner and Andy. The fact that he had bothered to exchange vehicles and purchase the necessary safety seats to keep her children secure impressed her even more than the fact that he trusted her judgment and complied with her rules for Tanner and Andy when the children traveled anywhere with him.

She shook her head as she smiled. "You certainly are full of surprises."

His brown eyes danced with obvious satisfaction. "All pleasant ones, I hope."

"Can we ride in Andres' new car, Mom? I mean, may we? Please?"

Andres raised his eyebrows in question, and Eve

shrugged. "Are you sure you want to fill up the back of that new vehicle with fifty pounds of cypress mulch?"

"Sure. Why not?"

She sighed. "I guess it's all right then."

"Great!" He lifted Andy from her arms and strode toward the shiny silver car.

"I'm afraid you'll have to show me how to adjust and secure all of the safety belts. The store clerk gave me a demonstration, but I barely understood a word she said."

The ride into the village of Buxton was brief and comfortable in the leather seats and air-conditioned interior of Andres' rented vehicle. From the front passenger seat, Eve directed him through heavy traffic along the main road of Hatteras Island to a local hardware and home improvement store.

After parking and unfastening the children from their safety seats, Andres put Andy in a shopping cart while Eve and Tanner walked beside them. They wandered up and down the aisles and browsed at beach furniture and fishing gear.

Finally, Eve glanced at her watch. When she turned toward Andres, she saw him already looking at her.

He tapped the brim of Tanner's hat. "Come on, *mi charro*. We'll shop for fishing line another time. We need to get back to the yard work." He smiled at Eve. "Where do we find the mulch you want?"

"In the gardening section, through that door to the right. I have to look for the kind Dad usually gets and then ask someone to carry the bags out to the car. I'll come back here to the register to pay."

Andres nodded. "I just want to look at some window locks."

"Oh?"

He gave her a reassuring smile. "I noticed that you have a couple of loose ones in the living room. I thought you might want to replace them."

She nodded and set her hands on the shopping cart handle. "I'll take Tanner and Andy with me."

"Aw, Mom. I want to stay with Andres."

She took her son's hand. "I need you to help me pick out the mulch. It'll take us just a few minutes."

Locating and selecting what she needed took longer than she planned. The kind of mulch her father usually purchased for the yards at the cottage was not included in the display with the other bags of mulch. Finally she found a clerk to bring the kind of mulch she needed from the warehouse behind the store, told him how many bags she wanted to purchase, and then explained where Andres had parked so the clerk could load them into the back of the vehicle.

By the time she hurried back to the registers, Andy was crying for a drink and straining to climb out of the shopping cart seat. Eve fumbled with the plastic latch of the child's safety belt with one hand while she searched through her purse for her wallet with the other.

"All set?"

Hearing his quiet voice with its charming Latin accent,

she looked up at Andres' smile, and in an instant, she felt a sense of calmness flow through her. She nodded and paid the cashier as Andres lifted the squealing little girl from the cart.

"Where's Tanner?"

Eve took her change from the cashier and closed her purse. "Right here." She looked around the cart and then made an actual circle at the end of the counter when she did not see her son. "I thought he was right here. Andres, where—?"

He set a hand on her shoulder. "He can't be far. Check the beach and fishing aisle. I'll take Andy outside and look for him there."

Panic rose in her throat as Eve rushed to the section of the store where they had been earlier. Not finding Tanner there, she headed to the mulch display, but again, she saw no sign of the little boy. Frantic, she asked every clerk she found, but no one had seen Tanner.

Her chest tightened, and her heart beat with pounding pressure as she ran through the front doors of the store and into the parking area. Her eyes scanned the numerous customers passing her as they entered and left the hardware store. Straining to see her blond, blue-eyed son, she forced her own eyes past the entrance to the cars in the parking area.

Her shoulders tensed at the sight of two dark compact vehicles in one far corner, and she could hardly breathe. The man who had been watching them had a dark car.

The stranger in black jeans and a fishing hat was not there, but his absence did little to calm her fear. Had the mysterious man taken her son when she was not looking?

Swallowing hot, humid air that almost choked her, she watched Andres wave a long arm at her. She shifted her gaze at the little boy beside him. Tanner was there.

Brushing past a group of people entering the store, Eve charged across the parking area and pulled the child into her arms. She covered his forehead and cheeks with kisses before holding him in a tight embrace. She squeezed him so hard that his hat toppled off and landed in the sandy lot.

"Mom! Will you stop that? What's going on?"

She felt the warm, comforting touch of Andres' hand on her back, and she raised her eyes to see a smile light up his handsome face. Had he been worried too?

She swallowed. "He was here all the time? Right by the car?"

Tanner squirmed from her arms and retrieved his hat. "I came out to help load the mulch." He brushed the brim with his small hand. "Then as the guy from the store was pushing his cart back toward the warehouse, a man with a fishing hat came over to talk with me. He had a rooster tail spinner stuck in the side, just like Grandpa does."

Eve's relief turned into instant terror. "A man?"

Nodding, Tanner set his hat back on his head. "He asked me about good fishing spots around here and the best kind of bait to use."

"You talked with him, Tanner? You talked with a stranger?"

The little boy's face paled. "I didn't think about that. He seemed so friendly. I told him about people catching big bluefish and flounder off the Avon Pier, and then he got in his car and drove off."

Eve grasped the child's shoulders. "Did he touch you, Tanner? Did that man try to take you away with him?"

"No, no, Mom." The child shook his head. "Really. He just talked with me."

She squatted before her son and studied his wide blue eyes. "Are you sure? He didn't hurt you?"

"He was nice, Mom."

"Tanner, never *ever* talk to someone you don't know. Promise me you'll never do that again."

Eve felt Andres touch her elbow and urge her to stand up next to him. "Your mother was just worried about you, *mi charro.*"

She inhaled a deep breath. "Talking to strangers is very dangerous."

"Not all strangers are dangerous, Mom. Andres was a stranger until we became friends."

"Don't argue with me, Tanner."

"Okay. Okay. I'd just like to know what's wrong."

Andres tapped the brim of the little boy's hat. "Nothing's wrong, partner. Go, climb into the car."

He leaned toward Eve. "He's all right. It wasn't his fault. Try not to upset him about what happened."

She stared up at the man with deep brown eyes and

chiseled cheekbones. "I can't help it. I'm worried sick about this."

The short ride home and the remainder of the afternoon passed with an unspoken tension between Eve and Andres. She was upset and needed to focus her anxiety on something concrete. That something just happened to be Andres Nunez.

She knew it was unfair of her to blame him for the panic and fear she had experienced when she discovered that Tanner was missing. After all, she had no proof that the stranger with the fishing hat had any connection at all with her daughter's father, but she could not help but suspect that his presence had resulted in the appearance of the unidentified man on Hatteras Island.

The fact that he had rushed into the house as soon as they arrived to contact the sheriff's office about the incident seemed to prove that he wanted to learn who the stranger was and stop his intrusion in their lives as much as she did. She knew she could trust Andres. She was just so upset about the incident at the hardware store.

Tanner clapped his hands together to brush off pieces of cypress mulch. "There. The yard looks really nice."

He smiled up at Andres who was grasping the wooden handles of the old rusted metal wheelbarrow they had used to distribute the mulch around the property. "Grandpa won't have to do anything when he gets here, except maybe mow the lawn again."

Eve pushed damp bangs from her forehead and

glanced at Andy, who was pouring sand from a measuring cup into a plastic bowl in the small sandbox near the steps leading to the back porch. "You've all worked very hard today." She raised tentative eyes to Andres. "Thank you for your help."

As he gave her a nod and a brief yet engaging smile, Tanner took her hand. "What's for dinner, Mom? I'm hungry, and thirsty too."

"I think we'll have a snack on the porch to hold us off till we get cleaned up. As dirty as we are, we can't possibly sit down at the dining room table."

"I'll just put this wheelbarrow in the storage shed, and then I'll watch Andy and Tanner while you get their snacks, okay?"

"You mean, we have to take a bath before we eat? Aw, Mom—"

She set a hand on his blond head. In the heat and humidity of the late afternoon, the child had decided, with his usual reluctance, to remove the beloved cowboy hat, the symbol representing to him everything noble, exciting, and masculine in his world that was so often full of maternal protectiveness and continued interruption of a younger female sibling.

"Yes, and I want you to scrub those fingernails."

"But, Mom—"

She shook her head. "Bath first, then dinner, but as a special treat, we'll have ice cream for our snack."

"Did I hear ice cream being mentioned?" Andres strode toward them and stopped to lift Andy, who was waving her hands from her perch on the edge of the sandbox, up into his arms.

"Make us big, tall cones with two scoops, Mom, because we worked really hard."

While Andres sat on the porch bench with Andy, Eve and Tanner entered the kitchen and washed their hands and faces. Then Eve pulled a quart of vanilla ice cream from the freezer.

Within minutes, she and Tanner had prepared cones for Andres and themselves and a small plastic bowl for Andy. With her son's help, she carried the ice cream and a pitcher of ice water and cups out onto the table on the porch.

As they ate rich, sweet ice cream, Tanner chatted with Andres about fishing and horses. Eve was amazed by the fact that the child seemed completely unaffected by his encounter with the strange man in the parking area at the hardware store. She, on the other hand, still felt her chest tighten with fear whenever she thought about the incident.

"Hey, there's my blue and white beach ball." Tanner stuffed the last of his cone into his mouth and chewed with furious speed. Swallowing, he pointed to a shady spot beneath a bunch of cedar trees. "I've been looking all over for that."

"It seems a little flat. Maybe it needs some air, *mi charro.*"

Tanner headed for the nearest set of steps. "That's why I didn't see it there, I guess. It's so flat." He glanced back and looked at Eve. "I hope you didn't run over it with the mower, Mom. I'll need it when we go to the beach again."

She shrugged tired shoulders. "No, I didn't, but that's the reason I remind you to pick up your things and put them where they belong."

Her son wrinkled his nose at her and then descended the wooden stairs. Eve's eyes moved from the little boy to Andres who was trying to wipe Andy's vanilla-coated mouth with a paper napkin while the little girl spun her head from side to side and squealed with disapproval.

"She's so dirty." Eve sighed. "Just look at her sun suit."

From his seat on the bench next to her, Andres met her eyes. "The child certainly enjoyed herself this afternoon."

"But we're all so grubby."

Smiling, he reached out and fingered a strand of Eve's hair that had escaped the elastic band at her nape. She held her breath as he tucked it behind her ear.

"I think grubby looks great on you."

Her heart jumped at his unexpected comment, and then she shook her head. "Don't tease me. I'm such a mess."

His brown eyes held her gaze. "I'm not teasing. You have an alluring, natural beauty that is very appealing."

She shook her head. "Don't." She experienced an immediate sense of disappointment as he dropped his hand.

"Don't what? Pay you a compliment?"

"Yes."

"Why not? Don't you know how to accept one?"

With effort, she pulled her eyes from him and glanced at Tanner, who had inflated his large beach ball and was now throwing it up into the air and catching it. "I guess, I'm just not used to getting one."

"That's a shame, my dear. In my opinion, a woman deserves sincere praise on a frequent basis."

She watched Andy scoop the last bit of her melted vanilla ice cream from her bowl. With care, she formed her question in her mind before she spoke. "Did you give Cheryl honest compliments?"

"I did, although I'm not sure she appreciated any kind of verbal tribute, especially regarding her appearance. By the time I met her, she was a beautiful, successful model recognized all over the world. She always had numerous enthusiastic admirers willing to sing her praises day and night."

"Were you jealous?"

He shook his head. "No. Even before we were married, I realized that Cheryl and I would lead a less than conventional existence as a couple. She was the one who pushed for marriage. I enjoyed her companionship and the excitement of her life when I was with her, but I never really belonged, and she wasn't able to change me, as she believed she could. I guess we were doomed from the beginning."

"What about love? Didn't you love each other?"

He raised his dark brows above searching brown eyes. "Does real love even exist in the world today? I'm not sure. Both my parents and my grandparents were in love, I know, but I haven't seen very much true love lately. Few of my colleagues and acquaintances are really happy in their relationships."

Andy held out her bowl, and Eve took it. "That's a rather pessimistic attitude. I believe that there has to be true love somewhere. Otherwise, why do we bother?"

"You sound like you're still searching." He leaned toward her and touched her arm. "Did you not love your husband?"

The question stunned her. She had not thought about Edwin in a long time. Talking about her deceased husband was uncomfortable for her, but she had asked Andres about Cheryl. It was only right that she give him the same consideration in answering his questions about her past marriage.

Swallowing, she stared at Andy's empty bowl. "I thought I did, and I believed he loved me."

"But?"

"But our relationship was never what I expected, I suppose."

"Mom! Andres!" Tanner's shouts interrupted her, and Andres pulled his hand from her arm as the little boy raced up the steps. "I'm getting hungry again."

Eve sighed. "Baths first, and your hair has to be washed too. When you're ready, I'll help you rinse out the shampoo."

"I want Andres to help me."

"No, Tanner—"

Andres smiled. "Let me help. In fact, I'll attempt to give the children their baths while you take yours. You deserve a little time to yourself."

"Aw, that'll take a long time. We have only one tub so we have to take turns. If Mom takes a bath too, we'll have to wait till midnight for dinner." The little boy shrugged. "Mom'll just have to take a shower likes she always does."

Andres met her eyes. "Well, let's see if we can take care of that little logistical problem."

"How? Hey, I know! Mom could take a bath in Mr. Wetmore's baby pool."

"Close, *mi charro*."

His brown eyes sparkled with obvious satisfaction that piqued Eve's curiosity and sent a silent warning somewhere in her mind. He pulled a key from the pocket of his pants.

"There is a huge sunken bathtub in the bathroom of the master bedroom. The tub has jets that send massaging streams of water in every direction. It's just waiting there for a grubby, exhausted mother to enjoy."

"Oh, no, I couldn't."

"Why not?" His quiet words challenged her.

"Because I have to scrub the children, help them dress in clean clothes, and get dinner started. I don't have time for a bath in a tub full of massaging jets."

"Your excuses are unacceptable."

"Unacceptable?"

He grinned, and her heart skipped a beat. Being near him seemed to cause unusual reactions in her body that she had never before experienced. Her mind raced, and her legs felt numb and unsteady.

"While I am sure I will not accomplish the necessary tasks as well as you, I certainly will try my best. If I do nothing else, I promise to keep your children safe." He winked at her. "Go. Enjoy yourself. Relax and soak in the tub. Tanner and I will do everything that needs to be done over here. Right, *mi charro*?"

Her son beamed. "Sure! We'll take care of it all, Mom. The baths, the clean clothes, the dinner." He wrinkled his nose. "I'll even scrub my fingernails."

Eve chewed her bottom lip as Andres grinned and dangled the keys in front of her. She wanted to decline his offer, but it was so tempting and so charmingly presented.

"I promise I won't let anything happen to Tanner and Andy. There will be two happy, clean, and safe children with me when you return."

She sighed. She knew they would be safe. She trusted the man who was her daughter's father. Despite the fact that she had wanted to blame him for the appearance of the strange man with the fishing hat in their lives, Eve's instinct told her that Andres would never let anything happen to Andy and Tanner or purposely put them in any danger.

Andres Nunez would protect her children. She was

confident of that, even if she was reluctant to relinquish her parental responsibilities to him while she enjoyed the luxury of a bubble bath.

"Go on, Mom. Andres will babysit for us just like Jaime Hasley does sometimes. And I'll tell him where everything is in the bathroom and the kitchen. I'll show him what to do if he needs help with anything."

Andres lifted her hand and pressed the keys into her palm. "There's a bottle of mineral water in the refrigerator. Pour yourself a glass and light a few candles and unwind." He brushed his fingertips along her jawline. "Take as long as you need, Eve."

"Candles? Andres, that's silly. We only use those when the power goes out. Doesn't the bathroom have a light?"

Eve watched the tall man reach out and tousle her son's blond hair. "She might not need candles, but I'll bet she likes them. Sometimes people find the glow of candlelight relaxing."

Tanner wrinkled his nose. "Lighting candles when you have electricity sounds mushy, like kissing."

Andres chuckled. "You're right, *mi charro*. Women like romantic things like candles."

"Like they like to boss us men around?"

"Well, yes, I suppose." He glanced at Eve and gave her a lopsided grin. "Let's get started with our jobs so your mother can go take her bath and get a little peace and quiet from all of your questions, okay?"

"Okay!"

Andres squatted and lifted his sticky daughter into his arms. "*Oh, niñita Rosita*, come along. It's time to scrub you up and find your pretty little face again."

The child bounced against him. "Noo-noo!"

"It's not *Noo-noo*, you silly girl. He's your daddy. Call him *Daddy.*" Tanner shook his head in irritation as he and Eve followed Andres into the house. "I don't think she'll ever get it right."

Eve watched Andres slip a long, tanned arm around her son's shoulders. "We have to have patience with her, *mi charro*. She's just a little girl, and she needs our help and direction so she can learn."

With Andy in his arms, he guided Tanner through the living room. "We are her family. It's our job to teach Andy what she needs to know to grow up to be happy and healthy and a good person who cares about others."

Eve stopped and waited as her children accompanied the handsome man with the captivating smile and Latin accent down the hallway. She smiled to herself. Tanner and Andy certainly liked Andres. She was happy to know that her children were comfortable with the man who was probably going to be a part of their family forever.

Andres cared about his daughter. Eve could see that, but he also cared about her son. She liked the way Andres always included Tanner in any conversation. She was the first to admit that, despite her son's numerous endearing qualities, his insatiable curiosity and continuous questioning were very often irritating to even the most patient adults; but Andres always responded to Tanner's questions with cheerful, good-natured answers, even though the little boy was not his own child.

He took care of both Andy and Tanner with love and concern. Eve appreciated the gentleness and obvious affection he had for the children he had not known existed a month ago.

Andres Nunez was an unusual man. Eve could not criticize his faultless treatment of her children, and as he considered their immediate needs, he also seemed to care about her. Her feelings and her opinions appeared to matter to him.

Andres was not the knight in shining armor of her dreams long ago that went running to her rescue. He was not perfect, of course, but he was emerging as someone who could be a trusting friend. Yes, a friend. She enjoyed having such a loving, caring friend in her life.

Chapter Six

After Andres had supervised the washing, shampooing, drying, and dressing of the two children in his charge, he acknowledged a distinct and newfound respect for all parents, including the green-eyed, auburn-haired woman whose impeccable child-caring skills were beyond reproach. The experience of seeing to the needs of Tanner and Andy without Eve's assistance heightened his awareness and understanding of her constant duties as a mother.

The children's energy level and desire for his full attention overwhelmed his sense of responsibility and forced him not only to see and appreciate Eve in a whole new light, but also to concede to a profound humility that he had never before experienced. Neither his training as a journalist nor his courage and perseverance in dangerous circumstances offered any guidance in the demanding challenges of child care.

With Tanner's eager assistance, Andres completed the tasks of bathing the children, as well as getting a good head start on dinner preparations before Eve returned from next door. The little boy and he were just putting corn muffins into the oven when she knocked on the door she had insisted Andres lock behind her when she left.

"That must be Mom." The child ran to the door. "I don't understand why we're locking everything up around here all of a sudden."

"Mm, something smells delicious." Eve stepped into the kitchen as Andres closed the oven.

"Mommy! Mommy!" Andy bounced in her seat at the table where she was playing with a stack of plastic measuring cups.

"We're making the meal that was Andres' favorite when he was a little *charro* like me." Tanner grabbed her hand and pulled her toward the stove where ingredients simmered in a large stainless steel pan on a back burner. "It's *poocho on caramel* something. It means beef stew."

Andres grinned. *"Puchero con carne de vaca."*

She raised green eyes to Andres. "I'm completely impressed."

His heart skipped a beat as he met her gaze. In the small kitchen, her presence was unmistakable. From where she stood, her scent drifted toward him; and when he inhaled, he did not smell beef stew or corn muffins.

He smelled only her clean, fresh, feminine fragrance mixed with the floral shampoo she must have used.

He swallowed and forced a smile. "This is the only meal I know how to make. It's a good thing you happened to have all of the ingredients to cook it."

"Things look completely under control around here."

Tanner bounced up and down beside her. "We just have to set the table and make a salad. Andres let me cut up all of the vegetables for the stew."

She set her head on his blond head. "I hope you were very careful with the knife."

He wrinkled his nose. "I was, Mom. You worry too much."

She nodded and looked back at Andres. "Maybe I do."

"Did you find everything you needed at the Wetmore house?' Andres could not stop staring at the woman who had just entered the kitchen. She had changed into a white knit sleeveless top and faded denim shorts. The tanned skin of her arms and legs appeared smooth and scrubbed, and damp wavy hair fell in thick tresses over her bare, sculpted shoulders. For a moment, he had a difficult time dismissing intense thoughts of combing his fingers through the long, curly strands.

"Yes, it was wonderful. I feel refreshed and clean again. Thank you for giving me time for such a nice treat."

He inhaled a steady breath and was acutely aware of how her quiet presence lit up the room and made him feel happy and relaxed. "Well, I'm going to run over and take a quick shower and change too. The muffins should be done in about twenty minutes."

Had he noticed how pretty and full her lips were or how her small freckle dotted nose wrinkled when she smiled? He felt as though he were seeing her for the first time.

She nodded. "Make a salad. Set the table. Take the muffins from the oven in twenty minutes. I think Tanner and I can handle that."

As the air in the galley kitchen seemed to close in on him, he took another deep breath and headed toward the door. When she stepped aside to allow him to pass, the mild fragrance of her floral shampoo floated past him. His knees felt weak and as though they were made of rubber. He had to get away from Eve Bennett. Without even saying good-bye to the children, he left the house and hurried down the steps and across the lawn.

Eve had been sincere when she told Andres she was impressed with everything he had accomplished while she had been luxuriating with selfish abandonment in a hot bubble bath at her absent neighbors' residence. The children appeared clean, safe, and content. The house itself was neat and orderly and without the pronounced level of confusion she had expected upon her return.

The simple dinner that Tanner had helped Andres prepare was tasty and nutritious. As Eve finished her meal, she sipped her water and stole a sideways glance at the man who was leaning toward her son discussing with great enthusiasm the casting techniques of various kinds of fishing line.

She had to admit that Andres Nunez had been more than a little helpful around the house that day. He certainly seemed interested and willing to be part of his daughter's life, but Eve wondered if he possessed the fortitude necessary to develop and sustain a commitment to Andy's upbringing.

A child needed a full-time parent, not one that popped in on occasion to take her to the park or out for ice cream. Parenthood was a serious obligation, and Eve could not, in good conscience, allow Andres to have a casual attitude about the important responsibility of raising the little girl she had grown to love, even if he was her biological father.

Her heart jumped when she felt him touch her arm. Her anticipation was edged with hesitation as she raised her eyes to meet his gaze.

The smile in his warm brown eyes caused her racing heart to skip a few beats that brought to her mind a sensation she had experienced long ago. The feeling had been a flutter of yearning when she had believed she was falling in love with her future husband, Edwin Bennett. Quickly, though, the subtle awareness of longing had dissolved into a quiet, comfortable, if mundane, sense of security created by marrying such a dependable and rational man like Edwin.

Exciting was not a word she would have used to describe her relationship with her late husband, but it was the best one she could use to depict the short time she had spent with Andres. In all honesty, the dark Latin man who was sitting next to her offered little in the way of reliability, and his risk-taking and impulsive behaviors were often far from prudent, but he definitely added excitement to her usual, ordinary life.

"Look."

His whisper pulled Eve from her thoughts. She followed his gaze to Andy, who had fallen asleep while still clutching her spoon in her tiny right hand.

"I think we finally tired her out."

Eve nodded and glanced at Tanner, whose eyes were also looking rather heavy. "I guess we all worked a little too hard today. I'll wash them up and put them to bed."

Andres stopped her as she rose from her chair. "Let me."

Eve inhaled a long, deep breath. She would have to get used to the idea of having Andres help her, at least with his little daughter.

She knew she trusted him. He had done an amazing job taking care of both Andy and Tanner while she was over at the Wetmore house. Her son adored him. Even little Andy, at times, chose Andres over her when she needed assistance or sought attention.

She lifted her gaze and looked into his deep, brown eyes. The combination of anticipation and eagerness made her smile. "Of course, go ahead. I'll clear the table."

"Come on, big guy." Andres urged the sleepy boy from his seat and then lifted Andy from hers. "Time for bed, children. It's been a very long day."

Without his usual fuss, Tanner accompanied Andres, with Andy asleep against his broad shoulder, out of the dining area. Eve sat for a moment as she continued to smile. So, it was definite. Andres Nunez was in her life for good, or at least, until Andy grew up and moved away from home. She would be listening to that quiet voice with the subtle Latin accent for many years. A little thrill of delight rushed through her mind at that thought. The realization made her smile wider than it had been, and she rose from her chair.

"There. All set." Andres strode into the kitchen where Eve was loading the dishwasher a few minutes later.

Although he had not used his cane all day, she noticed then that he was limping as he reached for the dishcloth next to the sink and headed toward the table. She wondered if he had done too much physical activity that day.

"Andy never woke up, and Tanner was asleep before his head touched the pillow." Andres wiped corn muffin crumbs into his hand. "Do you think they'll sleep through the night?"

She closed the dishwasher and pushed the power button. "Tanner rarely wakes until he's ready to get up in the morning. Poor little Andy will probably sleep straight through until lunchtime tomorrow."

She watched Andres rinse the dishcloth under a

stream of water from the faucet, wring out the excess water, and then drape it over the edge of the sink. As he turned toward her, he lifted a hand to push aside a strand of dark hair that had fallen across his brow.

He leaned against the cupboard opposite her and smiled. "Well, then, that should guarantee that you get a good night's rest." He reached across the space between them and brushed the knuckles of his hand along her right cheek. "You look so tired, Eve."

Her breath caught in her throat at the sound of his quiet remark. His words seemed so caring and kind. Swallowing, she pulled her gaze from him and opened the nearest cupboard door. "I think I'll make some coffee. Will you have some?"

His hand covered hers on the latch. "I'll do that."

"No." She shook her head.

He grinned. "Yes. Go sit down, and let me make you coffee."

When she hesitated, he eased her fingers from the door handle and gave them a gentle squeeze. "You trusted me with your children today. I know how difficult that must have been for you, but you did it with a gracious civility you were probably far from feeling. I appreciate that sacrifice, and I hope that someday I'll prove myself to be worthy of your respect."

He tucked a strand of wavy hair behind her ear. "For now, though, please allow me the simple pleasure of making you a simple after-dinner cup of coffee."

Eve felt as though she could not breathe. With extreme

determination, she forced air into her lungs and then re-gretted the action as the faint scent of his woodsy after-shave made his closeness even more evident than it had been a moment ago. She willed her heart to slow its er-ratic beat.

"Um, yes, I guess. Thank you."

He smiled and, settling his hands on her shoulders, guided her toward the dining area. "Go sit down in the living room and relax. I'll be there in just a few minutes."

Eve was arranging a pile of storybooks on one of the built-in shelves near a set of glass doors when Andres entered. She slid some more books into place and glanced up as he approached her.

"You're supposed to be relaxing."

"I will, as soon as I straighten up a little in here."

"Come on." He took a seat on the couch and patted the cushion next to him. "Stop working and sit down."

Sliding a large volume of nursery rhymes in a spot on the bottom shelf, Eve chose the upholstered chair where she usually sat in the evening after the children were in bed. As she looked toward him, she was not sur-prised that he was watching her.

"The stew was delicious. Is it an Argentine dish?"

He shrugged his broad shoulders. "I guess. My mother always did most of the cooking at the ranch, but when she and my father had to be away, my grand-mother took over in the kitchen. As I told Tanner, the *puchero* was my favorite. She used to make it frequently for my grandfather and me." He grinned. "Like Tanner, I used to help her cut the vegetables."

"You were an only child?"

"Not always."

She watched a shadow cross his handsome face, and for a moment he appeared to go to a place far away. He clasped the silver medal around his neck with the long, tanned fingers of one hand. While she waited for him to continue, she sat in the sudden silence that filled the air with only the drip of the coffee maker to disrupt the stillness.

When he met her eyes again, his were overflowing with an expression she thought she recognized as grief. She could not help but wonder what had happened to cause such emotional pain.

"I had a younger brother, Luis, but he died."

She thought she should go to him and comfort the sad, quiet man on the couch, but she remained in her chair. "I'm sorry, Andres."

"It was an accident. Luis was four, just a baby. I was ten, his big brother. My parents took his death especially hard. I'm not sure my mother ever fully recovered from her grief. I remember her crying for months and months after he was gone."

"I'm sure the loss of a child is devastating for a parent. I can't imagine the sorrow your mother and father experienced. The thought of losing Tanner or Andy is absolutely terrifying to me."

He exhaled a deep sigh. "Mom and Dad were never the same after Luis died."

Although her curiosity was aroused, Eve did not press him to give her any details regarding his little brother's death. It was obvious to her that the subject was a difficult and disturbing one for him.

He appeared to force a smile as he leaned back against the couch. She studied his chiseled cheekbones and the horizontal lines etched across his forehead. It was not hard to imagine him in a saddle riding a proud stallion as it galloped along a southwestern desert trail.

"Tell me about Edwin."

His words astonished her. "Edwin?"

"Yes, tell me about Tanner's father."

"I already told you about him."

"I know only that he never gave you compliments."

"He gave me compliments." She clasped her hands together on her lap. "Just not the kind you were talking about."

"What kind did he give you then?"

"Well, he always said that I was a good cook and that I kept the house clean and neat." She imagined his brows lifting above questioning brown eyes, but she refused to look at him. "Edwin was a practical man."

"It sounds like he married you for your housekeeping and culinary skills."

"You don't know anything about him."

"Tell me."

She sighed. "The topic of this conversation is making me very uncomfortable."

"Does Tanner look like him?"

She nodded. "He had Edwin's coloring, but that's all. Tanner never knew him. Edwin died of stomach cancer five months before Tanner was born."

"I'm sorry, Eve."

She squeezed her hands until her knuckles turned white. "Edwin didn't want children. I didn't realize until we were married how adamant he was about the idea of not having a child. I always hoped that he would learn to love his son, but he died before he had the chance."

Andres leaned forward and covered her tightly folded hands with one of his. "I'm sure he would have grown to love Tanner. The child is irresistible."

The tears that clouded her eyes were not for Edwin or even for herself. They were for all the opportunities her son had missed sharing with his father and all the times Edwin had lost with his son.

"It must have been very difficult for you, raising a child all alone."

She raised her eyes then to look at him as he sat back on the couch. "I wasn't really alone. I mean, my parents have always been very supportive. Tanner has never lacked male role models in his life. My father, my brothers, and my sisters' husbands are all very close to Tanner."

"It's wonderful to have such an involved extended

family. Mine was like that too, when I was growing up. There were always aunts, uncles, and cousins living all around us."

"Does your family still live in New Mexico?"

He sighed. "When I was fourteen, my grandfather died. Four years later, my father died of a heart attack. A year later, my mother died of complications from pneumonia. My grandmother passed away a few years ago while I was on assignment in Kosovo in Eastern Europe. The only close relatives I have left are my aunt and uncle who run the ranch now, and a few cousins scattered around the country pursuing their various careers."

"Just like you? Traveling around the world in search of adventure and excitement? Never calling anyplace home? Is it the blood of ancient Spanish conquistadors that keeps you from settling down and being satisfied with a quiet, well-ordered life?"

A grin tugged at the corners of his mouth. "Maybe. I've never liked the idea of settling for a boring and ordinary existence. Fast and chaotic is my preferred lifestyle."

A low buzzing sound interrupted the conversation, and Eve watched Andres pull a telephone from the waistband of his pants. He glanced at the display screen and then at her.

"Excuse me for a minute. It's the sheriff's office."

The sheriff's office. She had almost forgotten about the stranger with the fishing hat. Swallowing a sudden wave of fear, she nodded and rose to her feet. "I need to go and check on the kids, anyway."

Wanting to listen but being too afraid to stay, she hurried from the living room and down the hall toward the bedrooms. Andres would share the details with her, if there were any to share. Was she overreacting about the man lurking around the house and following them in the village? Maybe he was just a tourist asking about fishing in the Outer Banks, as Tanner had presumed. Although she would be reluctant to admit it aloud, she was relieved to have another adult involved in the mysterious situation.

Being a responsible and self-reliant single parent all of the time could be overwhelming. Sharing such an awesome job with Andres, despite his lack of obligation to a typical family life, gave her a sense of security.

After finding both of her children asleep and then adjusting the air-conditioning temperature of each room so they would not get too cold during the night, Eve went to the kitchen and poured two mugs of strong black coffee. Andres was just finishing his call when she entered the living room once again.

He set the cellular telephone on a nearby end table and accepted the cup she handed him. "I was supposed to be serving you tonight."

She sat on the edge of her chair and tried to balance her mug on shaking knees. "Have the police been able to find out anything about that man in the fishing hat?"

Andres took a sip of hot liquid and then settled back

against the couch cushions. "Not much, I'm afraid. After I called them this afternoon and reported the incident at the hardware store, the police use the description to track him to the Avon Pier."

"So he was telling Tanner the truth? He really was interested in going fishing?"

Andres took another drink from his mug. "Apparently so."

"What did he tell the police? Why has he been watching us?"

He shook his head. "I'm afraid he slipped away before the deputy could question him."

Disappointment knotted in her stomach. "I was hoping the police would find some kind of clue to explain the man's strange behavior."

"The deputy wasn't able to speak with the guy, but he did get the license number of the vehicle he was driving."

"The license number? That's good, isn't it? I mean, the police locate people all the time with license plate numbers."

He nodded. "It's a start."

"Well? What did the police find out from the license?" She felt impatience creeping into her voice. Why was he taking so long to tell her? Was there something about the stranger that he did not want to share with her?

Andres set his coffee mug next to the phone on the end table. "The car is registered in Virginia. If it's not stolen, and the police found no report that it was, then the man's name is Albert Clement of Manassas."

She caught her bottom lip between her teeth and repeated the name to herself. Finally, she exhaled a heavy breath. "I don't think I know anyone by that name."

He leaned toward her and held her gaze. "Albert Clement? It doesn't sound familiar to you?"

"No, it doesn't." She felt irritation replace her impatience. "Should it?"

"I don't know, Eve."

"What about you? Do you recognize that name? Who do you know in Manassas?"

He shrugged broad shoulders. "A few casual acquaintances. Fellow journalists. No one close to me. No friends that I know of live in or near Manassas. The name sounds completely unfamiliar to me."

"Well, who is he then? Why is he watching us?"

"According to the police, Albert Clement is a private investigator by profession."

"A what?"

"A detective hired—"

"I know what a private investigator does. I just can't believe that one is investigating us." She felt her eyes narrow at him. "What have you done, Andres Nunez?"

"Me?" His brown eyes grew big and round, and when she saw the expression of sheer astonishment on his handsome face, she immediately wished she had not used such a harsh tone to ask her question. She was just so anxious about her family's safety.

"I haven't done anything here that warrants investigation by a private detective." With apparent impatience, he brushed back from his tanned forehead the strand of hair that insisted on falling forward. "As I've said before, I see no reason for you to accuse me of any improprieties, especially any that would cause someone to hire an investigator to follow me."

She sighed, and some of the frustration she had been experiencing ebbed away. "I'm sorry, Andres, Forgive me." She squeezed her mug. "What could he want, then?"

Andres shook his head. "I have no idea. The police are continuing to look into his business and personal life."

With trembling hands, she raised the ceramic cup to her lips and took a long, slow drink of coffee. The strong liquid felt like an acid in her stomach that churned in nauseous waves she could not calm. *A private detective. What does he want?*

Her life was orderly and quiet and ordinary. Private investigators worked in movies and mystery books. They were not a part of her life or the lives of her children. She tried not to allow the panic she felt to rise in her throat.

"The police want to speak with Tanner."

"Tanner? Why?"

"Because he's the only one who has actually had any contact with Clement. They think he may be able to provide some insight into why this guy is hanging around here."

"Tanner has no insight. He's just a child."

"The police think that by having him review the conversation he had with Clement, Tanner may remember something he hasn't told us about this man."

She gave her head a firm shake. "Absolutely not. I won't have my son subjected to—"

He held up his hand to stop her. "That's what I told the deputy on the phone. Alarming the boy will do no good, especially since I doubt that he can help at all to identify the man's reason for being here. I believe Tanner's been completely open with us about the whole incident."

Andres leaned forward and took her coffee from her hands. After setting the mug next to his on the end table, he folded her trembling fingers in his large, tanned hands. Warmth from his touch flowed up her arms, and she shivered.

"I agree with you that keeping the situation low-key for Tanner's sake is the best way to protect him, but he is a smart child, Eve. He is going to figure out that something is happening. He already has questions about the locked doors. You are going to have to decide how to handle the child's natural curiosity regarding this issue."

He rubbed the pads of his thumbs along her knuckles, and she felt a little of her tension ease. She raised her eyes to find those kind, concerned eyes looking back at her. "You can't protect him from everything forever, Eve."

"I have to." Her whispered words revealed her apprehension and frustration. "I'm his mother."

His thumbs continued their slow, caressing movements on the backs of her hands. "You are a wonderful mother, but it's your job to help him face problems that come along. You cannot hope to control everything in his life. You can only help him handle what happens when it does."

He gave her a slight smile and released his hold on her. "Despite his mysterious behavior, Albert Clement does not seem to be trying very hard to be inconspicuous. He wears that big, wide-brimmed canvas hat with artificial lures dangling from it. Although he has eluded our attempts to follow him, he sticks around this small island and makes several appearances in public places throughout the village."

Andres sighed and rose to his feet. "I know it's probably difficult for you to believe, but Albert Clement does not appear to have any malicious intent. If he did, he would have taken Tanner in the hardware store parking lot this afternoon. He had the opportunity, but all he did was talk with the child."

An exclamation of sudden fear escaped from her lips as Eve recalled how close the stranger had been to Tanner. She found little comfort in Andres' words.

Clasping her elbows, he urged her up from her chair. He gazed down at her before he spoke. "I promise you that we'll figure this whole mess out, Eve. You will have your quiet, ordered life back again soon."

She held her breath as he drew her into his arms. She felt his muscles flex as he rubbed his hands up and down her back before pulling her into a close embrace. She enjoyed the support of his nearness and allowed the comfort of his arms to soothe her after a few moments. She felt herself begin to relax as he helped to relieve the fear that had threatened to overwhelm her.

Clearing her throat, she stepped away from him. "I'll get us more coffee."

He shook his head as he dropped his long, tanned arms to his sides. "No more for me. I've had enough, thank you. I think it's time for me to leave."

She nodded. "Yes, it's getting late."

Of course Andres had to leave. Even though the last topic of conversation had been rather disturbing, she had enjoyed his company that evening. She appreciated having the opportunity to spend time with another adult. It was fun to have someone with whom she could share a grown-up conversation.

"You have my cell number." He walked through the kitchen to the door he always used. "You'll call if you need anything?"

She smiled and held the screen door open. "I won't need anything."

In the porch light, his brown eyes leveled on hers. "But if you do, I'll be right over. Secure the lock on this door as soon as I leave, okay?"

"I will. Good night, Andres."

Eve did not sleep well that night when she finally slipped between the sheets of her bed and closed her eyes. Concern about the stranger with the wide-brimmed hat still plagued her, although she acknowledged that she was not as nervous as she had been the first night she noticed him lurking around the neighborhood. She did not need to go check on the children every half hour throughout the night or jump at every bump or rustle she heard outdoors. Andres had managed to alleviate some of her worries.

Of course, she wondered what possible interest a private detective would have in her or her family, and she ultimately concluded that her intuition was right. Andres must be mistaken. *He* had to be the subject of the stranger's investigation, not her. Now that the police had a license number and an address, she felt confident that it would not be long before they discovered the truth.

With those thoughts easing her apprehension, she tried to drift off to sleep, but she found that rest was still elusive. Visions of Andres filled her mind. His quick smile, his soothing words, and his deep, quiet Latin voice accented images of his tall, muscular body striding toward her or stooping to pick up Andy or leaning down next to Tanner to share a joke or a comment.

Her numerous attempts to rid her thoughts of him were useless. His soft laugh drifted in and out of her mind and mixed with thoughts of sharing family dinners and working side by side with him while completing typical household chores.

In spite of her efforts, she could not forget Andres. He was there in her mind, in her life, and in her heart.

Her heart? She definitely had to be careful. He had an allure that was hard for her to resist, but resist she must. No good could come from developing more than a casual relationship with him, not for her or for her children.

If he followed his usual schedule, he would be gone the next day and a half, at least, back to Washington. Maybe that was good. They all needed time to settle into their own routine again. She needed time to catch her breath. Andres always made her feel as though she were spinning in some kind of emotional whirlwind whenever he was near her. Wondering when she would see him again, Eve drifted into a restless slumber.

"Please, Mom, I'm so thirsty. I really need some orange juice."

Eve glanced at Andy on the living room floor and watched the little girl push a small plastic truck up and down the arm of a nearby chair. "Have a drink of water, Tanner," she said as she brushed her feather duster along a row of bookcases.

"Aw, Mom." Holding a large orange in his hand, the little boy stood in the dining room leaning against a broom. "I need something more than water. I need juice. I think I'm going to faint from being so thirsty."

"We'll make juice after we finish the chores."

"Why doesn't Andy have to do chores? It's not fair."

Sighing, Eve turned toward her son as the little girl made truck noises in her throat. "She's two years old."

"So. I'll bet you made me clean when I was two years old."

"Tanner."

"Well, anyway, the house probably didn't get as dirty with just the two of us. Now that there're three people, we should all help out. Andy messes things up too."

"You know that your sister is too young to help."

"She can sweep. She's got her own little broom."

"Tanner, be sensible. You didn't sweep the floors when you were two."

"I think seven is too young to sweep floors too."

"I'm not arguing with you. Go finish the kitchen floor."

The child kicked the tiles with the toe of his sneaker. "I wish Andres was here. He makes work fun." His blue eyes brightened. "May I call him, Mom?"

She sighed again. "Of course not, Tanner. We don't even know if he's home."

"Where else would he be?"

"That's none of our business, is it?" She started dusting again. "Now, let's get back to work."

A knock at the side door made her jump. The sound created a knot of nervousness in her stomach.

"Hey, Mom, it's Andres. He's here!" Tanner had pushed the curtain away from the window in the upper half of the door. "Hey, it's locked again. Why is this thing always locked? Hi, Andres. Am I glad you're here!"

Eve's heart raced as she heard Andres' quiet voice and appealing Latin accent as he greeted her son and entered the house. Andy's squeals of excitement filled the air.

"Noo-noo's here, Mommy? Noo-noo's here?"

"Good morning, *mi charro*. I hope you slept well last night."

The way he rolled his *r* sounds toward the back of his throat made her breath catch in her own, and Eve swallowed. She followed Andy as the little girl stumbled into the kitchen in a hurry to greet their visitor.

"You came just in time to save me." Tanner tossed the orange into the air. "Mom's really cranky again today."

Eve watched Andres lift his eyebrows and set a hand on her son's blond head. She noticed that he was not using his cane, and his thick dark hair was damp, as though he had just taken a shower. With his navy T-shirt tucked into faded jeans at his narrow waist, he looked ready to go fishing or hiking or horseback riding. In silence she wondered why he had not gone to Washington.

"Now, Tanner, perhaps your mother has a good reason for not being as cheerful as usual. A headache, maybe? Or a bad dream?"

Her son wrinkled his nose as he tossed the orange into the air with one hand again while holding the broom with the other. "I don't know why, but she's very cranky right now. She won't even let me have juice."

Andres caught the orange and then scooped Andy into his arm. "I'm sure your mother has a good reason for that too."

"She says I have to sweep the kitchen floor first."

"Well, let's get that done." He met Eve's gaze. "And then maybe she'll let us squeeze some juice for everyone."

With a long sigh, Eve stepped back into the living room and continued her dusting. *If Andres wants to babysit, let him.*

As long as he did not interfere with her authority as a parent, she had no valid reason to stop him from spending time with his daughter. If he wanted to keep Tanner and Andy occupied while she did housekeeping chores, she would welcome his assistance.

She had just pulled the vacuum cleaner from the storage closet when she heard a peel of children's laughter. A shout from Tanner and a squeal from Andy piqued her curiosity, and she rushed through the dining area. She reached the kitchen just in time to see her son use the broom to sweep an orange toward the laundry room doorway where Andres was squatting next to Andy. The little girl held her own plastic toy broom while Andres helped her to stop the piece of fruit from rolling between the door jams.

"Score! I made a goal! Did you see that, Andres? I did it!"

"Would someone like to explain what is going on out here?"

Tanner spun around to her as Andres and Andy looked up from the focus of their attention, the orange on the floor. Silence hung in the air. Tanner moved to stand closer to his conspirators and then shrugged his thin shoulders.

"We're sweeping, Mom. See?" With his hands, he brushed the broom back and forth across the floor in front of him. "Even Andy is helping, and you said she was too little to sweep."

Eve set her hands on her hips and glared at the one adult of the group who was giving her a sheepish and attractive grin. "I think you've done enough sweeping for this morning. Pick up the orange, Tanner, and then put the brooms away."

"Aw, Mom—"

"Tanner."

"Okay, okay. I'm going."

Eve waited until her son had taken Andy's toy broom to her room before she narrowed her eyes at Andres. "What do you think you're doing?"

He rose to his full height and lifted Andy into his arms. "Now, Eve, we were just having a little fun. We did no harm."

"You were playing with food."

"We didn't even break the peeling."

"I doubt that it's still edible."

"I'll pay to replace it."

"That's not the point."

He sighed. "What is the point, Eve? We were just having a good time." He grinned at her again. "You're not opposed to fun, are you?"

"No, but I don't allow my children to play soccer in the house."

His dark eyes gleamed. "It wasn't soccer. It was hockey. Fruit-and-broom hockey, to be exact."

Eve pressed her fingers to her temples. "I don't care what it's called. It's not allowed in my kitchen."

He gave her a look of exaggerated astonishment. "I'm afraid I have to agree with Tanner."

She felt a headache beginning to throb at her nape. "About what?"

"You are a bit on the cranky side today."

"Oh, you . . . you big kid!" She balled her hands into tight fists at her sides. "You're no more mature than a seven-year-old."

His smile only added to her irritation. She inhaled a deep breath and tried to ease the tension in her head.

"If being mature means not having fun, then I don't want to be mature." He kissed the top of Andy's curly head. "When my daughter grows up, I hope that being mature doesn't stop her from having a good time."

"Hey, I've got a great idea!" Tanner darted into the galley kitchen and skidded to a stop in front of Eve. "We should go to the beach after lunch."

"Today is a work day."

"But, Mom, we worked all day yesterday. If we get all of the chores done now, why can't we take a break and go to the beach later?"

Eve chewed her lower lip as Andres' brown eyes

watched her. The housework was almost completed, and they *had* worked hard the previous day in the yard.

She was not sure why she was reluctant at the moment to give into the idea. She often took the children swimming, and the hot, sunny weather was perfect for spending an afternoon at the beach. Was her hesitance influenced by Andres' teasing smile and coaxing words? Did the irresponsible behaviors of the charming man who was standing in her kitchen holding her daughter in his arms have anything to do with influencing her indecisiveness?

"Please, Mom, it'll be fun."

"Yes, Eve, going to the beach sounds like fun—and we all think you need to have some fun."

With a sigh, she opened her fists and rubbed the palms of her hands on her shorts. Finally, she shook her head and smiled. "All right. You win. We'll go to the beach as soon as we have lunch."

Chapter Seven

"**M**om won't take us to the ocean side. She says the waves are too rough." Tanner had made a continual verbal commentary from his seat in the back of Andres' car ever since they had left the house.

Neither Eve nor Andres, who was driving, responded unless the little boy asked a specific question that warranted an answer. He did not appear to require a verbal reply from them. Andy fell asleep in her car seat beside the chattering youngster.

"She's right about the waves. Grandpa took me surf fishing once, and a wave came straight up on the sand after me. The ground under my feet slipped away all at once, and the water took me with it out to sea. It was really scary."

Eve recalled the day last summer when her father

had insisted on taking Tanner fishing. She watched the little boy lose his balance and then disappear under the water's surface as she sat on the beach with Andy. She had nightmares for over a week about the incident. Her imagination soared with possible tragic conclusions, and she had then decided to protect Tanner and Andy from the perils of the ocean by taking them only to the sound side of the island for swimming and other beach activities, unless there were several family members with her to help her watch them and keep them safe from the powerful surf waters.

"Turn left at the next sign, Andres. This is my favorite beach on the sound side. The water is warm and calm and really shallow for a long way out. I can walk forever and still touch the bottom with my feet. And there are so many shells. Andy loves to pick up shells, but I have to help her sort them out. Sometimes she finds broken ones and wants to keep them. If you look carefully, you can find perfect shells. I always tell Andy that a perfect shell is much better than one with a crack or a piece missing from it."

Tanner strained against his seat belt as he twisted to look between Eve and Andres to get a view through the windshield. "Wow! Look at all of the cars, Mom. The parking lot's never this full. Everybody must be taking a break today."

Andres pulled the vehicle into a space at the end of a row of cars and turned off the ignition. "It looks like that's an empty spot on the beach to the right over there, but we'll have a long walk to reach it. Are you up to helping carry some gear, *mi charro*?"

The child grinned. "Sure, I am. I'll get my chair and the blanket and the bag of towels. Andy can carry the pails and shovels, and Mom can carry her. You can get the other chairs, and then we can come back for the boogie boards and the umbrella."

"What about the cooler with the drinks?"

"We usually keep that in the car and just come back if we need a snack. Mom says if we do it that way, the food and bottles don't get all sandy."

"That sounds like a good idea." Andres smiled. "Your mom thinks of everything, doesn't she?"

Eve unhooked her seat belt and turned to watch Tanner nod. "That's because she's a mom. They're supposed to know what to do."

Although Eve tried to avoid Andres' probing dark eyes, she was unable to resist his gaze. She met it as he released his own safety belt and pivoted around in his seat toward her.

His smile broadened. "Your mom is a very special woman, *mi charro*."

"She's okay, I guess." Tanner scrambled from the restraints of his booster seat. "Let's get going. I want to swim."

Eve wanted to pull away from the invisible hold Andres seemed to have on her. His intense eyes darkened, and his expression grew serious as he studied her.

Without warning, her heart began to race. Her mouth

grew dry, and a quivering sensation fluttered in her stomach. Time stood still as the connection between them gained strength. What was happening? She did not want to identify the feelings that she had for the impetuous, high-spirited man who insisted on planting himself right in the middle of her life. He was a friend, a good one, but just a friend.

"Come on! What are you waiting for?" Tanner's insistent voice filled the enclosed space of the vehicle.

Eve was aware of Andy stirring in her car seat while she felt unable to move at all. With difficulty, she swallowed the dry lump in her throat.

To her relief, Andres finally pulled his gaze from hers and smiled at Tanner. "Right, *mi charro*. Let's go. We need to get this car unloaded."

Despite her initial reservations about going to the beach, the afternoon proceeded with unexpected pleasure. The delightful summer weather and the change in setting away from the cottage, where she was always tempted to do work of some kind, provided a sense of contentment and rejuvenation that surprised her.

Sitting in a low chair under the umbrella where she could watch Andy play in the sand and Tanner and Andres splashing in the water, Eve felt completely unperturbed She stretched her legs out in front of her and wiggled her bare feet in the warm sand.

Andy tossed her a grin as Eve watched the little girl scoop sand and shells with a small shovel into a plastic pail and then dump it out, only to start all over again.

Her eyes roamed to the water's edge where Tanner's blond head and Andres' dark one leaned closely together as though they were studying something either on the surface or under the water.

When Tanner lifted his head and saw her, he waved with a wide, gesturing arm. "Hey, Mom, come on in! The water's so warm!"

She wiggled her toes again and shook her head. "No, I'm perfectly happy right here."

Andy giggled and tried to catch Eve's toes as they disappeared in the soft, white sand. "They're gone."

The little girl dug with her shovel in a frantic attempt to uncover her feet. "I find them, Mommy."

"Find what?" Tanner shouted as he bounded toward their little piece of beach. "Look, Andres. Andy thinks Mom's feet are lost. What a silly girl!"

Loping along the sand, Andres dropped into the chair next to Eve and gave her a broad smile. "You're missing all the fun. Why don't you go and take a swim. I'll watch the kids for a while."

She shook her head. "I'm having a great time right here."

He raised his eyebrows. "What? Having fun? The quiet, solemn Eve Bennett is actually having fun?"

She wiggled her toes as they reappeared again with Andy's diligent digging.

"I've been known to relax occasionally." Glancing at him through the dark lenses of her sunglasses, she returned his smile.

He tipped his head and continued to study her. "I do believe that *sandy* and *relaxing* look just as good on you as *grubby* does, but it's a very close call."

His teasing tone made her heart jump, and she pulled her eyes away from his handsome, angular face. Without planning to do so, she shifted her focus to the jagged red scar on his upper thigh.

"How's your leg doing today?"

He hesitated, and she wondered if he would refuse to answer her. After a few moments, he looked away across the smooth, blue waters of Pamlico Sound and sighed.

"It's all right at the moment. When I was in the water, the warm temperature felt good, but the pain never goes away completely. I'm not sure it ever will."

"Plodding through this sand probably doesn't help. You should be walking on a solid, level surface and wearing good, supportive shoes."

He raised his eyebrows as she watched the rebellious strand of dark hair fall across his forehead. He pushed it away with the back of his hand. "You sound just like my doctor. He wants me to lead a cautious, boring life too."

"Cautious and boring from your perspective, maybe. Such precautions are appropriate and necessary for your recovery." She used her most stern and professional voice but felt a grin spread over her face. "I'm beginning to understand that if an activity is not slightly dangerous, then it's boring to you."

He kicked sand with the toes of his right foot. "I just

want the stupid leg to get back to normal. I want to be able to get around the way I did before that car bomb exploded. I want to do everything just like I used to . . . without a cane."

As she listened, she tried to empathize with him. The man was unbelievable. Despite the perilous life he led, his attitude regarding his health and welfare was almost childlike in its simplicity. His lack of acceptance of his own vulnerability amazed her.

With his arm, Tanner reached toward her. "Ow, Mom. I got sand in my eye."

"Come, let me see." She gestured to her son who was covering one eye with his other hand.

"I'm going over to the bath house to wash it out with water from a faucet."

"No, Tanner, not by yourself. I'll come too."

"Aw, Mom. You always let me go there by myself. What's going on?"

Eve glanced at Andres before turning her attention back to her son. "You might need help washing out your eye."

"I don't need help, but I do need to wash it out now. It really hurts!"

Andres jumped up from his seat. "I have to wash some sand off too, *mi charro*. Can you show me how the faucets work over there? I can't seem to get the water to stay on."

"Sure. Come on."

Eve watched the two run together toward the wooden

enclosures surrounded by a concrete platform with several outdoor benches, spigots, and drains where beach-goers could rinse off sand and salt water before climbing into their vehicles for the ride back to their hotel or residence elsewhere on the island. She smiled as Andres squatted next to her son and attracted Tanner's complete attention with some entertaining remark or humorous comment that she could not hear.

Andres Nunez. He always seemed to come to her rescue just when she needed help. He was like a child himself with his reckless behavior and carefree attitude, but he appeared to know just what to do to distract or protect her children when a problem occurred. Not only was he insightful regarding the children's care, he also seemed to know what she was thinking and that she was worried about Tanner going off on his own.

Until she had a plausible explanation of Albert Clement's presence, she did not wanted Tanner to wander too far away from her, but of course, the persistent, independent little boy could not simply allow her to accompany him. By nature, he would have to protest, even with the discomfort of sand in his eye.

Andres had solved the potential problem with a smooth and natural excuse to escort her son so that Tanner could show him how to use the faucet. She could not ignore the feeling of warmth and admiration she felt for the tall, Latin man who seemed to fit so well into her family.

"Pick me up, Mommy."

Eve forced her attention to Andy who was tugging her arm. "Pick you up? Are you finished playing in the sand?"

When the child nodded, her dark brown curls bounced in all directions. "I'm so tired, Mommy. I want to rest."

Eve smiled and patted her legs. "Come, sit on my lap, sweetie. We'll both rest awhile." She drew the child into her arms and cuddled the damp and sandy girl against her.

"Mom! Mom!"

The urgency in Tanner's voice made Eve's heart race. She stared in the direction of the bathhouse and saw her son hurrying toward her.

"Tanner, what is it? Is your eye still hurting?"

"No, no. Look at Andres!" He pointed to their handsome, dark companion trotting in the direction of the parking area, appearing to be in pursuit of another individual. "He saw that man from the hardware store taking our picture. You know, Mom, the one with the fishing hat."

"He had a camera this time?"

"Yes, and Andres was really mad and yelled at him. He tried to grab the camera but couldn't get it before the man started running. Andres told me to come back to you."

Eve thought her heart would burst from her chest as she watched a small car speed out of the beach parking lot with a squeal of tires. Several moments passed before Andres turned and headed back across the sand toward them. He walked with slow, labored steps, and there was a noticeable limp in his gait. It took all of Eve's effort not to rush over to him and help him back to a chair, but she knew that such an action would wound his male pride. He did not accept assistance with grace.

Andres' tanned face was tight with visible strain, and the white line along his jaw told her he was upset, as well as determined. She swallowed the lump of fear forming in her throat.

"Why was that man taking pictures of us, Andres?"

Eve glanced at Tanner's bright face, full of curiosity and questions. Her son was unaware of the possible danger of the situation or that she was fighting to conceal her distress and growing panic.

"He was probably just a tourist snapping photos of the beach." Her voice was low and shaky. "Why don't you take Andy and collect a few more shells before we pack up and go home? We saw some pretty ones over next to Andy's red pail."

She waited until the children were several feet from them before she dared to speak again. Her mouth felt dry as she met Andres' dark eyes. "Now pictures? Oh, Andres, why is he doing this to us? What is going on?"

He shook his head and dropped a plastic film canister into her lap. "Mr. Clement was not in a talking mood, but fortunately, in his haste to leave, he dropped this container on the ground. Maybe it holds a clue to his behavior."

"Undeveloped photographs? How will these help us understand why he's been lurking around us?"

She watched him shrug his broad shoulders. Beads of perspiration glistened on his forehead. The skin of his tanned face was taut.

"I don't know. They might not help at all. I'll get the film developed as soon as we get back to Buxton."

He closed his eyes and grimaced. It was apparent to Eve that he was experiencing extreme pain from the exertion of his run. He should not have chased the stranger who had been taking photographs of them. Walking on rough ground and shifting sand was bad enough, but running was even worse. She hoped that the physical effort of pursuing the private investigator had not caused any permanent damage to his injured leg.

"I think Andy and Tanner have had enough sun for one day. I'll start packing up so we can head back home."

He opened his eyes and gave her a slight smile. "We don't have to rush. Albert Clement is gone now. I doubt if he will bother us anymore today."

Rising from her beach chair, she brushed sand from a towel and then folded it. "You're probably right. I'm more concerned about you at the moment."

"Me?" He lifted dark brows above wide eyes full of surprise as she handed him a folded beach chair and slid the handles of a canvas bag full of towels and beach towels onto her shoulder. "What about me? You do not need to worry about me, Eve."

She folded another chair. "Someone has to. *You're* certainly not doing a very good job of it."

Giving her a sheepish grin that sent her heart into a racing rhythm, he nodded toward Tanner and Andy who were running across the sand toward them. They giggled and chattered about the shells they had found.

"Okay, we'll leave, Nurse Bennett, but not because I need to go. We'll go because I can see that those two children are getting tired."

"Right. The children."

She pulled the umbrella from the sand and pushed the button to collapse it into a manageable size. "I'll take a load of stuff to your car and then come back and help with Tanner and Andy, okay?"

She watched his grin fade while the skin along his jaw tightened. He clutched his left leg as another spasm of intense pain appeared to rake through it.

Her chest tightened as she imagined how much he was suffering. "I think I'd better drive."

Nodding, he closed his eyes for a moment. "I guess I won't argue with you."

Eve studied his anguished expression and fought the urge to offer a few words of empathy, but she was not sure how he would react. She would have reached out to squeeze his arm or to give him a hug if she thought he would accept such a comforting gesture, but she was sure the action would embarrass him and add to his discomfort.

One of his endearing smiles relaxed the tautness of his face. "We should get the kids home. They look very tired, don't they?"

Shaking her head, she smiled back at him. "You are unbelievable, Andres."

When he winked at her, she held her hand out to Andy. "Come with me, sweetie. We have to take these things to the car. Tanner, stay here and help Andres finish picking up the chairs and toys."

"I'll watch her."

"No." She shook her head. "If she runs, you'll have to catch her, and you don't need to harm your leg anymore than you already have. Don't try to be a hero, Andres. Stay here with Tanner until we get back, okay?"

As he hesitated, she met his dark brown eyes. His teasing expression disappeared as the uncooperative strand of hair fell across his forehead again.

"You don't always have to be so strong, you know. No one is infallible." She kept her voice low so that Tanner would not hear.

With obvious reluctance, he nodded and brushed the strand of hair back from his frowning face. His broad shoulders dropped as he heaved a sigh and appeared to force a smile. "Okay, *mi charro*, let's collect these things so we're ready when your mother and sister get back."

In less than thirty minutes, Eve pulled Andres' vehicle into the Wetmore driveway and turned off the ignition. Looking at the man in the passenger seat beside her, she saw that his tanned face was strained and edged with discomfort. Her chest tightened as she acknowledged her helplessness in easing his pain. Without considering the consequences, she reached across the console and set her hand on his arm.

"Do you think you need help to get inside?"

His smile barely went beyond his mouth, and his exasperation over the situation was clear. "I can manage. Thanks."

Eve refused to allow him to injure himself more just because of silly masculine arrogance when she could see that he was in a great deal of pain. She glanced at the children in the rearview mirror. "Tanner, I'll be right back. Stay in your seat."

She opened the driver's side door and stepped onto the shell and crushed stone drive. Rounding the front of the vehicle, she reached Andres as he stepped onto the ground.

"Where's your cane?"

"In the house."

"Then lean on me." She slid her arm around his waist as he took some unsteady steps in the driveway.

"Eve, this is really not necessary."

Lifting her eyebrows, she remained silent and refused to remove her hold on him. Standing so closely to him, she realized how big and tall he actually was. She knew that, if he chose to reject her assistance, he could push her aside and wobble across the lawn and up the front walk on his own.

After a few seconds of initial impasse, they turned together and struggled toward the Wetmore house. Eve watched his jaw tighten and his face contort with every step.

Supporting his large frame was a challenge that required all of her strength and concentration. By the time they reached the front door, she was out of breath, and she had to wipe beads of perspiration from her forehead.

"I'll be all right now, Eve." His voice was breathless as he clutched the railing with both hands. "Go take care of the kids. I'll unload the car later."

With her arm still around his waist, she smiled at him. "Tanner and I can do that. We'll even vacuum out the sand."

This time, he did not even attempt to protest. She gestured toward the front door. "Do you have a key to get in the house?"

Nodding, he took one hand from the railing and slipped it into the front pocket of the short-sleeved button-down shirt he had pulled on over his boxer swimming suit after leaving the water. He dangled the key from its plastic key ring.

"What about pain medication?"

"What?" His eyes mirrored intense pain as it raked through him once again.

"Medicine from your doctor for your leg. Do you have some?"

"Oh, yes. A pain reliever and an anti-inflammatory pill."

"Would you like me to get them for you?"

He shook his head. "I think I left the bottles on the kitchen counter."

"Take some, Andres, and lie down right away. You need to rest your leg."

With her hand still pressed against his lower back, she rubbed it up and down his spine. His shirt was damp with perspiration, and she felt toned muscles flexing beneath her fingers as he inserted the key into the lock before stepping into the hallway.

Her heart skipped a beat as she stood next to him, and heat seemed to close in on her despite the rush of cool air flowing from the house through the doorway. She inhaled a deep, unsteady breath and swallowed. "Get some rest, Andres. I'll call you later."

"Mrs. Bennett! Mrs. Bennett!"

Eve looked up from the picnic table where she sat next to Andy and across from Tanner at a village ice cream shop. A tall, thin teenager in nylon shorts and a tank top approached them.

"Well, hi, Jaime. We haven't seen you in a long time."

The young woman tossed a straight strand of blond hair over her shoulder and patted Tanner on the brim of his cowboy hat. "It's my summer job. Mom and Dad said I have to pay for my own car insurance if I want to drive, so I'm working almost thirty hours a week."

"You have another job, Jaime? I thought your job was babysitting us."

"It used to be, Tanner, but now I have a new job." Jaime Hasley grinned at the little boy and then lifted Andy into her arms. "I might even have to miss Mom and Dad's neighborhood barbecue this year. It's next Saturday. You're going, aren't you?"

Eve caught a drip from Andy's chocolate ice cream cone before it fell onto Jaime's blouse. "Of course. We always have such a good time."

"You're not working now," Tanner said. "Why don't you come and play at our house for a while? We miss you, Jaime."

The teenager grinned and turned to Eve. "I'd like that, if it's all right with you, Mrs. Bennett. I'm all finished at the shop for today."

"We'd love to have you come, Jaime. I just need to make a quick stop at the photo store, and then we're heading home."

Jaime kissed Andy's ice-cream-coated cheek. "Okay, I'll follow you in my car."

A few hours later, Eve tucked the packet of developed color photographs that she had picked up in town into her purse and hurried across the grass toward the Wetmore residence. She was worried about Andres. She had tried to call his cellular telephone twice, but he had not answered. He had not arrived for dinner as she had hoped, and it had been several hours since she had left him at the front door after their trip to the beach. His car was still in her driveway where she had left it after unpacking and vacuuming it.

As she climbed the wide wooden steps leading to the first floor of the house, she appreciated her good fortune. Jaime Hasley had offered to stay with Andy and Tanner while she went to check on Andres.

Eve's chest tightened as she rang the doorbell and then knocked. No one answered, and she could hear no movement from within the multi-story structure.

What could have happened to him? Was the damage to his injured leg worse than she had suspected? Had he fallen and struck his head? Was he lying unconscious somewhere in the house?

An endless list of possibilities ran through her mind, and very few of them had favorable ramifications. Her palm was damp as she turned the doorknob. Already racing, her heart pounded so hard she thought she heard it beating. The knob twisted and the door swung open. Willing her heart to slow down so that she could listen for any sound that would indicate Andres' whereabouts, she stepped into the dark, quiet foyer.

Familiar with the layout of the first floor, she proceeded to check nearby rooms. To the left was a doorway to the large living room where the rope and wood bridge hung suspended from the open beam ceiling. It was empty. To the right, there was a formal dining room, and next to it was a library with shelves of books, a desk, and a computer. Both rooms were also unoccupied.

With racing thoughts, she moved toward the back of the house to the kitchen and master bedroom. For a brief moment, she recalled the previous afternoon when she had taken the same path to the bathroom adjacent to the bedroom and had enjoyed a long, relaxing bath. Andres had insisted that she take time for herself while he watched the children and made the preparations for dinner. She had been surprised and delighted by his gesture of such kindness.

Inhaling long, slow breaths, she hoped that he had taken a hot bath when they had returned from the beach and was now sleeping in the bedroom. Apart from her obvious concern for his health, she could not figure out why she possessed such an intense need to check on him and make sure he was doing okay. Certainly a strong, independent individual like Andres Nunez was used to taking care of himself.

She stood in the doorway of the bright, spacious kitchen and large center island, plenty of counter space and cupboards, and a dining area next to glass doors leading to the first-floor deck that overlooked the grass-covered back lawn and calm waters of Pamlico Sound beyond it. Along one side of the rectangular oak table stood, instead of chairs, a long wooden bench. It was there that she found Andres.

From across the room, Eve stifled an exclamation of astonishment and relief as she watched him. He seemed to be asleep with his broad shoulders propped up against one end of the unpadded bench. His head rested on the narrow top of it while his long legs, tanned and sprinkled with dark curly hair, were stretched out along the bare piece of furniture, almost reaching the opposite end.

Aside from the fact that he appeared completely uncomfortable, he *did* seem to be resting. Eve noticed that he was still wearing his swimsuit and the shirt he had slipped on with it for the ride home from the beach. The untied sneakers he had been wearing were overturned on the floor next to the bench as though he had kicked them off and had allowed them to drop from his feet right there at the end of his seat.

Why had he not gone to the bedroom to lie down? Had he slept for hours in such an awkward position? If he had, he would be stiff and sore in more places than his left thigh when he awoke.

As Eve debated in silence about whether or not she should wake Andres, he began to writhe and mumble in Spanish. She did not understand his words, but she could tell that he was agitated or upset in some way. His voice rose in volume, and his movements became more erratic.

She held her breath and worried that he might fall off the bench. His distressed shouts became louder and more insistent.

"No, no! Luis, no!"

When he thrashed against the back of the bench, she thought he would injure himself further and rushed to his side. Putting the envelope of photographs on the table, she set her hand on his broad, muscular shoulder.

"Andres, wake up. You're dreaming."

When he continued to twist and groan, she grasped him with more force and shook him until he began to awaken. Huge and round, his dark brown eyes stared at her for several long moments. With slow, jerking movements, he dropped his legs to the floor and pivoted to sit up against the back of the bench.

Eve reached out and brushed his tanned forehead with her fingers. "Are you all right?"

She watched him swallow as he continued to look at her. He appeared to be returning from someplace far away.

"What time is it?"

She glanced at her wristwatch. "A little after eight. Have you been sleeping here since we got back from the beach?"

"The beach? Oh, yes." He rubbed the side of his neck and winced. "It's after eight? I guess that pain medicine really knocked me out."

She shook her head. "You shouldn't have slept so long on such a hard surface."

He stretched his neck and rubbed the toned cords along its length. "I have a terrible cramp in my neck."

"How's your leg?"

He brushed his left thigh with the palm of his hand. "Better, I think, but still really sore. I can't believe that chasing Clement across the parking lot could make it hurt so much. I guess I won't be running in a marathon anytime soon."

"Why didn't you go right to bed, Andres?"

She watched him drag a hand through his thick, dark hair and then push aside the strand that was always falling over his forehead. Her heartbeat accelerated as a grin tugged at the corners of his mouth.

"I didn't plan to stay here so long. After you helped me to the door, I was too exhausted and too sore to take a shower and change, but I was all gritty and sandy from the beach. I didn't want to crawl into bed like that, so I thought I'd just lie down here in the kitchen and rest for a while."

She shook her head. "But now you have a stiff neck as well as a sore leg, and you were very restless. Something seemed to be bothering you while you slept."

He looked away from her. "I guess I was dreaming."

"It sounded like a nightmare. You appeared to be very upset."

He rubbed his neck again. "I don't think I've had a good night's sleep since that unfortunate car bomb blew my leg apart."

"I thought maybe those were the memories that were bothering you, but then you called out a name."

"A name?"

"Luis."

A faraway expression that she had seen in his dark eyes when he had first awakened returned. It appeared to her that he was daydreaming again. She placed a hand on his shoulder.

"Luis was your little brother's name, wasn't it?"

His dazed look appeared to transform in slow motion

from bewilderment to awareness, and he blinked. "I called out Luis's name?"

"Yes, you were speaking in Spanish, I think. Has your younger brother been on your mind lately?"

"I don't know." He shrugged, and Eve felt his muscles stretch and compress against her palm.

"Not consciously, anyway, but maybe Tanner's questions about home and New Mexico have triggered some memories." He glanced around the kitchen before leveling his eyes on her. "Hey, where are the kids?"

"Over at the house with Jaime Hasley, our babysitter. She stopped by to visit for a while."

"Hasley? Like the real estate agent?" A shadow crossed his face. "You told her to be sure to keep the doors locked?"

Eve nodded. "Yes, I told her. We met Jaime in the village when we went to get that roll of film developed, and Tanner invited her to stop by this evening."

She watched him as he dragged a hand through his hair. His handsome face was so drawn that concern tumbled in her stomach. She reached to retrieve the envelope of photographs from the table.

"I almost forgot about that film. How did the pictures turn out?"

"You were right. He was photographing us." She slid the pile of glossy pictures from the protective paper pouch and handed them to him. "Most of them are of Andy. There are a few of you and Tanner, but the majority of them are of Andy and me."

He flipped through the entire pile once in silence and then took time to scrutinize each photograph. Finally, he looked at her. "Mr. Clement seems to be especially interested in her, doesn't he?" His gaze drifted to the set of pictures on his lap. "I wonder why."

Eve folded her hands together in front of her and squeezed until her knuckles turned white. "I've been trying to come up with a plausible explanation. You don't suppose he's making plans to kidnap her or to do something terrible like that, do you?"

He pulled his gaze from the top picture on the stack and met her eyes. "Eve, come on. Don't do that to yourself. You have to try not to imagine the worst."

Stretching out his free hand, he pressed her arm with gentle fingers. "You're going to drive yourself crazy worrying about this guy."

"I can't help it." Her words were a hoarse whisper. "I've never had to deal with such a situation. I'm just not sure how I should act."

He urged her toward the bench. "First of all, you have to stay calm and try not to be so pessimistic."

She allowed him to pull her down onto the seat beside him. "But you're still worried. Even though you chased him away from the beach today, you're still concerned about his lurking around here. You asked me if I reminded Jaime about locking the doors."

He turned so he could look at her and then smiled. "I am being cautious. We can be attentive without letting this whole bizarre state of affairs rule our lives." He rubbed one of her palms with the pad of his thumb. "You don't strike me as a gloom-and-doom type of person, Eve Bennett. You are always so cheerful and upbeat."

Despite her distress over the photographs, she returned his smile. "Not always, at least, not according to Tanner. He's called me cranky on more than one occasion recently."

His thumb made tiny circles against the sensitive skin of her palm. His touch was both comforting and mesmerizing.

"Ah, yes. I have a suspicion that the child may have contributed to your frustration and irritation. I am afraid we men sometimes inadvertently infuriate the women we love without even realizing we're doing it. I guess it's one of many masculine shortcomings."

Finally he released her hand and lifted his to touch her chin. With gentle fingers, he tipped her head and gazed down at her. "We're going to find out why Albert Clement is hanging around and taking pictures. I promise, Eve. We'll get through this mysterious situation together, okay?"

She swallowed the lump that had formed in her throat. His face was so close to hers that she could feel his breath fan across her cheek. Awareness of his undeniable physical proximity caused her heart to race and confused her thoughts. She felt lightheaded as she tried in that instance to identify what role this dark, handsome man was now playing in her life.

Her feelings for him were strong, but she hesitated to

identify them. She was starting to care about him very much. She wanted to be with him whenever they were not together.

Dragging in a long, deep breath, she nodded. In silence, she took from him the pile of pictures and replaced them in the envelope on the table.

"I can't believe how sore my neck is."

After securing the flap of the photo packet, she watched as he again rubbed the side of his neck with his hand. When she saw him wince, her chest tightened in compassion.

"Here, let me help you." She rose and rounded the end of the bench. Standing behind him, she set her palms on his shoulders.

She used her fingers to knead his skin and the cords of his neck. As she worked her way up and down, he sat very still and did not say a word.

After a few minutes, she felt the tightness of his muscles start to relax in response to her gentle, methodical movements. She sensed his gradual relaxation and release of tension.

Her fingers trembled, and she had a hard time concentrating. Just as she thought that she would not be able to finish the simple massage, she felt his shoulders flex beneath her fingers. To her surprise, he reached up and covered her hands with his.

"That feels so much better, Eve. Thanks."

Chapter Eight

Eve took a few steps away from the bench and tried to calm her racing heart. She inhaled a deep breath and cleared her throat. "Do you think you can walk well enough to get to the shower now?"

As he nodded, she rounded the end of the bench to face him. "Hold on to my arm for balance while you try to stand."

She watched his brown eyes darken and could not tell if he was giving her a nonverbal expression of uncertainty and frustration over his physical condition or if the sudden shadow was a manifestation of some other intense emotion. Trying to concentrate on his injury, she pushed away the now familiar feeling of enjoyment and comfort she had began to experience whenever she was with Andres.

Using the end of the bench for support, he rose with slow, unsteady movements to his feet. The grimace on his face told her that he was still in a great deal of pain.

As beads of perspiration formed on his forehead, he reached out and set his hand on her shoulder. "Oh, this is definitely not going to be good."

"It's okay, Andres. Sit back down." She helped him ease himself back onto the bench. "You'll just have to use your cane."

He dragged a hand through his already disheveled hair, and her heart jumped as she looked at the vulnerable expression on his handsome face. She blinked.

"Where is it? I'll get it for you."

Bending at his waist, he rubbed his left calf with both hands. "The cramps are gone, but the muscles are still so incredibly sore." He shook his head. "And all because of a little run across the beach parking lot."

"Not to mention the days of abuse you gave it without proper rest or support, right?" She sighed. "Are you going to tell me where your cane is, or do I have to search the whole house for it without your help?"

He stopped massaging his leg and raised his dark eyes to her. "I'd like to forget where I put it. I hate that stupid thing."

Exasperation washed over her as she put her hands on her hips and stared at him. "That stupid thing is what's going to help you get better, Andres Nunez. Are you telling me that you're going to allow your stubborn Latin pride to prevent you from using your cane and actually help your leg to heal?"

His brown eyes widened. "It's not pride, really. It's—"

"It's pride, male ego at its best. You think you're invincible. You think you're some kind of super being, better and stronger than your fellow humans. You've convinced yourself that you can survive in this world without help or support."

He pushed a strand of hair back from his forehead. "That cane is a stigma."

"A what?"

"A stigma. A mark or symbol of weakness."

"That's ridiculous. It's a piece of wood, not a sign that one is lacking vitality or worth." She took a seat beside him on the bench and grasped his hand. "Andres, I can't believe you'd even think that foolishness. You are an intelligent man. You must know that such reasoning makes no sense."

His look of distress melted her heart as he squeezed her hand. Despite her irritation at the careless behavior that had caused his current health misery, she could not rid herself of the strong desire to console and reassure him. He looked so miserable sitting of the bench next to her. He was no longer the invincible man he thought he was.

She sighed and forced a smile. "Now you listen to me, Andres. You have to be positive about this whole thing. Look at Tanner. He thinks you're some sort of Old West hero who's appeared in his life to befriend and entertain him. Your leg injury only adds to the mystique of your presence."

He nodded and slapped his leg. "Some hero."

"You *are,* to him, and to Andy too. What if she gets injured one day and has to use crutches or a wheelchair or some other means of assistance? Wouldn't you want her to do what she should to get better again?"

"Yes, of course. I love her and want the best for her."

"Don't you want to teach Andy that her health is more important than personal vanity?"

He gave her a slight smile. "You're right, but—"

"But what? Rather than directing all of your anger and frustration at your cane, you should, perhaps, reevaluate the choices you've been making in your life."

"My choices?"

"Your recklessness. Your lack of caution. Andres, you're a thirty-two-year-old father, and you're still running around the world seeking out the most dangerous places and situations you can find and then putting yourself in terrifying circumstances."

"I am an investigative reporter. It's what I do. I go where the news is."

"You don't have to do it all. You have other responsibilities now. Your daughter needs you, alive and healthy. Maybe it's time for you to consider a career change."

He shook his head. "I can't do anything else."

"You can't, or you *won't*? I think you're addicted to the thrill and danger of overseas assignments, of living on the edge, facing life-and-death situations every day. You enjoy that rush and stimulation."

"It's my job."

"It's more than a job to you, Andres, and that kind of self-indulgence was fine when you were young and alone, but now you have a daughter. Andy has to come first. She matters more than the next news story you can get in some remote part of the world."

He dragged a hand through his hair and pulled his eyes from her to gaze around the kitchen. After several long moments, he said, "I think I left it by the bed."

"Left what?"

"My cane. It's in the bedroom."

She squeezed his hand and rose from her seat. "Don't move. I'll be right back."

Hurrying from the kitchen, she followed the short hallway to the master bedroom and found the cane propped against the nightstand. She grabbed it and returned to the kitchen.

"Thank you." His voice had a grudging tone as he took the wooden stick, the symbol of his disability, from her grasp.

Without waiting for him to insist that he did not need her help, she slipped her arm around his waist to steady him as he rose to his feet. His legs wobbled, and after glancing down at her, he set his arm on her shoulders and began to take slow, small steps toward the bedroom.

By the time they crossed the bedroom floor, Andres' shirt was damp with perspiration, and she noticed he was breathing harder than he had been in the kitchen. "You'd better have a seat on the bed for a few minutes before you take your shower."

The fact that he did not argue told her that his pain was intense once again. "It's probably time for you to have more medication. I'll get you some water."

He pulled a plastic prescription bottle from the pocket of his swimsuit and fumbled with the protective cap. Eve could see that his hands were shaking.

Touching his arm with her hand, she reached for the pills. "Let me do that."

She entered the large, adjacent bathroom where she had enjoyed her delightful bubble bath the previous evening and filled a glass with water from the sink faucet. Returning to the bedroom, she removed a tablet from the medication bottle and handed both the pill and the water to Andres.

She rubbed his shoulder as he emptied the glass. "Are you going to be able to manage a shower by yourself?"

Despite his obvious discomfort, he raised deep brown eyes to her. "Yes, I'll be all right. Fortunately the Wetmores have designed their house to be both handicap accessible and user-friendly. There are bars for support on the sides of the shower stall and even a molded seat in case one needs to sit." He sighed. "I may have to."

He looked so tired and drawn. She wanted to reach out and hug him. Instead, she inhaled a long breath to steady her nerves and forced a light note into her trembling voice. "Are there clean towels in there, or should I find some for you?"

Shaking his head, he smiled. "Go. I can take care of myself."

She shook her head. "I'm waiting until you're done. I want to make sure you're relaxed and safe before that pain reliever starts to take its full effect on you."

Without an argument, he rose and allowed Eve to help him into the bathroom. After making sure that soap, shampoo, towels, and a change of clothing—as well as his cane—were within his reach, she returned to the bedroom. While she waited for him to finish, she wandered around the large room with a wall of sliding doors that overlooked the calm waters of Pamlico Sound.

The scene was peaceful as she watched a red kayak with a lone rider skim along the surface of the water in the brilliant light of the North Carolina sunset, but what she felt inside was far from serene. Being near Andres, she found, was becoming more and more complicated.

She realized that she was attracted to him. She could not deny that fact, but she knew she had to be careful about how she responded to the ever-increasing feelings of wanting to be with him and to share not only her daughter but also all other parts of her life with him.

Movement in the room pulled her from her contemplation, and she turned from the windows. Crossing the floor, she went to Andres and helped him sit down on the edge of the king-size bed.

"There. How does that feel?"

"Wonderful." He closed his eyes for a moment after he propped himself up against some pillows. "You're right. I should have done this when I first got back here."

Chewing her lower lip, she sat in the chair beside the bed and met his eyes with a direct gaze. "Now, you need to rest, Andres. I mean, really rest. You need to sleep."

With drooping eyelids, he looked at her and nodded. "I don't think that will be a problem. The medicine is already making me drowsy."

"And I don't mean just for now. You have to rest and relax for the next several days. You need a great deal of recuperation so your body can start to heal. Promise me you'll take it easy and not push yourself again until your leg gets better."

He reached out to entwine his fingers with one of her hands, and her mouth went dry. She inhaled a quick breath.

"No more running or doing yard work or even playing broom and orange hockey in the house. You need absolute rest."

She felt the pressure from his hand increase, and she swallowed. "When you have to walk, you'll need to use your cane. You'll need it all the time, not just when you think no one is watching you."

He gave her a teasing grin. "Yes, Nurse Bennett."

"I'm serious, Andres."

"Very serious, it would seem."

"You should call your doctor too, and describe your symptoms to him. I'm sure he'll want to see you as soon as you're well enough to make the trip back to Washington."

"If I didn't know better, I might think that you're trying to get rid of me."

"Absolutely not. In fact, in my opinion, you should have complete bed rest for at least a week."

"A week? In this house?" He shook his head. "I could never stay away from Andy for so long."

Eve nodded. "I'll bring her here, but you'll have to promise not to lift her or chase after her."

"And what about Tanner? He wants to give me another fishing lesson."

She narrowed her eyes at him. "Only if you sit in a comfortable chair on the dock in the backyard and fish right here in the canal. No surf fishing or fishing off any kind of pier or boat."

"Did anyone ever tell you that your serious side is not very fun, Eve?"

"You don't need fun; you need rest." She squeezed his hand and set it next to him. "Now go to sleep."

He caught her hand in midair. "Stay for a while."

"I should be getting back."

"Just a few minutes more."

"Now you sound like Tanner when he wants me to keep reading and not turn off his light at bedtime."

"I don't want a story. I want a song."

"A song?"

"Sing to me, Eve. Do you know any slow, romantic country songs with a happy ending? You look like you enjoy country ballads with happy endings."

She studied his glassy eyes for a few moments and thought the pain medication he had taken must be taking effect because his speech was beginning to ramble. "I don't think so, Andres."

She set his hand back on the bed. "You need to get some sleep."

"My grandmother used to sing to me."

"That's very nice. I'm sure she sang wonderful songs to you."

"She never refused when I requested a song."

"I'm not your grandmother."

He closed his eyes and then opened them again an instant later. "But you have many of her qualities. She was a very nurturing person too."

"I'm sure she loved you very much."

"Have I ever told you how great you are, Eve?"

"Go to sleep, Andres."

"No, I mean it. You're an exceptional mother and a wonderful person. And you have a natural attractiveness." He reached up and held her hand once again. He moved his fingers in gentle caresses over hers.

Eve's breath caught in her throat. She tried to unwrap his hand from hers.

"You don't have to work at being beautiful. You just are."

"Andres—"

"Have I ever thanked you, Eve? For all you've done for Andy? I should thank you—"

His words faded as his hand dropped to the mattress and his eyelids closed. Soon, his deep, steady breathing told her he was asleep, and she took quiet, unhurried steps from the room. Her hand still tingled from his touch.

To Andres' extreme impatience, his injured leg required over a week of bed rest to return to the point of recovery he had reached before he made the irresponsible choice of chasing Albert Clement across the parking area the afternoon he accompanied Eve and her family to a nearby Hatteras Island beach. Just as she had predicted, his doctor insisted that he remain in bed as much as possible and not travel during the entire time.

He should have been irritated by her assertiveness regarding his personal health, but instead he found himself comforted by her concern and attention. Her behavior actually stirred up feelings that caused him to want to provide her with the same kind of care and help she had shown him, if ever she needed it.

True to her word, she packed up Andy and Tanner every day and crossed the yard between the Wetmore house and her own family's cottage to visit him. The little group arrived with a bag of food for meals and snacks, another full of toys and storybooks, and another of extra clothing in case the children needed to change.

It seemed to Andres that the members of the Bennett family were practically living at his house during the hours that he was awake, but he was also aware that when he was sleeping for long periods of time, Eve took the children back to their own home where they lived their lives without him. Sometimes that thought left him with a sense of loss that he had never experienced before. There was an awareness of separation and isolation that he could not explain.

Was it loneliness? Why did he feel lonely when he was not with Eve's family? He had spent most of his adult life alone, with only his work to keep him company. Why did he want, at that point in his life, to be with others, and not just others in general, but with Andy and Tanner and Eve?

The need defied reason, of course. Did he really want to be with the two-year-old with a thirty-second attention span and a seven-year-old with a boundless supply of both energy and questions? Did he want to be with a bossy, rule-following nurse who was not afraid to give him her opinion about his choices in life?

Yes, he wanted to be with them. He wanted to spend time with them. He wanted to share their lives. He wanted to be a *part* of their lives.

"Andres, my boy. It's good to see you. Where have you been?" Perry Reilly, the senior editor of *Washington Today,* approached his table at the busy Arlington restaurant.

Smiling, Andres rose and shook the gentleman's outstretched hand. "Good afternoon, Perry."

The silver-haired man patted him on the back and then took a seat across from him. "Thank you for taking time to meet with me. I haven't had a day off in weeks. We have a number of positions to fill because several people are retiring or transferring to our offices in Europe."

His boss picked up the menu on the table in front of him and continued. "Although we've hired many new journalists, they're young and confident and ambitious. They think they have to travel to hot spots all around the world to write the best stories and to prove themselves."

Andres took a drink from his water glass as the older man smiled. Trying to be patient, he restrained his curiosity about the lunch meeting his editor had requested earlier that day.

"As a result, the Washington office has openings in several departments at this time, but that fact doesn't concern you, does it, Andres? Do you know when your doctors will be signing your release to return to work? We're anticipating your coming back within the next few weeks."

Andres set his glass on the table. "The physical therapy is going well. I had a small setback a little over a week ago, but if I don't do too much strenuous activity, I should be able to accept my next assignment by the middle of August."

"That's great. It's good to hear you're recovering and that you'll soon be back writing for us."

His editor met his eyes. "I think you'll be glad to know that Roger Walton has decided to take a couple of years to concentrate on his book about recent Israeli-Palestinian terrorist activities. He wants to stay in Tel-Aviv, but we need someone to take his place, someone to travel in that area and get the news as it happens. Roger is going to be too distracted with his manuscript to fulfill his obligations to the magazine. What do you think, Andres? Would you like to cover the West Bank for a year or two?"

"What?" Andres stared at the senior editor as his mind raced. The West Bank. Palestine. It was the assignment of his dreams. "Are you serious?"

Perry Reilly leaned forward in his seat. "I thought you'd be pleased. The paperwork is all in order. We're just waiting for your medical releases. Of course, all your doctors will have to give their permission for you to return to work."

For a moment, there was silence at the table as Andres allowed himself to become accustomed to the astonishing announcement of his next assignment. Now that his leg was beginning to feel better, he had noticed experiencing a sort of restlessness that he attributed to the need to return to work, but he had started to think about returning to Baghdad, not to Israel, where he had wanted, for years, to go.

The senior editor chuckled. "It looks like your vacation is ending, and you now have some big decisions to make."

He nodded as a collection of thoughts about the future rushed through his mind. Reporting the news from Palestine was the job of a lifetime, his dream coming true. It was the assignment for which he had always longed.

The ring of the cellular telephone in the pocket of his pants jarred him from his silent reflections and growing exhilaration. "Excuse me." He nodded to the man sitting across the table from him. "I'll be right back."

As he headed for the lobby of the restaurant, he checked the incoming number displayed on the screen. He recognized it immediately. It was Eve's home phone.

"Hello, Andres? Is that you?"

"Yes, *mi charro*. Is everything okay?"

"Sure. I just wanted to let you know that there's a John Wayne movie on television tonight. It's a Western." Tanner paused. "I thought you'd want to know. Maybe you'd like to watch it there while you're in Washington."

"John Wayne?" Andres felt relief wash over him. "Oh yes, if I remember, I'll probably turn it on when I get back to my hotel room. Are Andy and your mom okay?"

"Yup. Mom's right here. She wants to talk with you."

Andres held the phone to his ear as he took a deep breath and waited. He could not help wondering during those few seconds if something was wrong.

"Hi, Andres. I'm so sorry about this interruption." Eve's breathless voice filled his ears. "I put your number on speed dial, and Tanner pressed the button before I could talk him out of calling you about the movie tonight."

Speed dial? My number's on your speed dial? He could not explain why he found that thought so appealing.

"You're not interrupting. I was just having lunch with my editor. Is there a problem?"

"No, no problem. Tanner's just excited about the showing of several John Wayne Westerns on one of the classic movie channels this week. I tried to explain that you were probably too busy to watch television, but he insisted that you'd want to know."

"Well, tell him I appreciate the call. You are definitely all okay?"

"We're fine. I put Andy down for a nap a few minutes ago, and Tanner and I were just relaxing in the air-conditioned quietness for a while. We did yard work all morning, but it's very hot here today. We're resting indoors, out of the oppressive afternoon humidity. How are you feeling?"

"Better than ever. Physical therapy went well this morning." The idea occurred to him that he should share his wonderful news with her, that he should tell her about his next assignment.

"That's good to hear. Well, I'll let you get back to your lunch. Oh, wait. Tanner wants to speak with you again, if you don't mind."

"No, put him on."

"Andres, guess what?" The little boy's voice was full of excitement. "I caught a croaker off the dock, a really big one. Mom helped me clean it, and then we put it in the freezer. We can have it for dinner one night when you get back."

"That's great, *mi charro*. I've never had croaker before."

"It's delicious, as good as sea trout. Hey, Andy just woke up. She wants to talk with you too."

"Hi, Noo-noo."

"*Hola,* sweet, little *niñita*. You must have had a very short nap."

"No more sleeping. I play now. Daddy play too?"

Before Andres could respond, he heard Tanner in the background. "Daddy has to work. He can't play with us right now. Maybe he'll come later."

Then the little boy spoke into the telephone. "Andres, we have to go. Mom says we can't bother you anymore. Please, come back soon. 'Bye."

"Good-bye, *mi charro*."

For a long time after the call had ended, Andres stood near a stand of regional newspapers and magazines in the busy restaurant lobby and replayed the conversation in his mind. Finally, he smiled to himself.

If anyone had told him two months ago that he would be enjoying a discussion about fishing and old Western movies with a seven-year-old John Wayne fan or listening to the happy giggles of a two-year-old instead of having a serious conversation with his editor about future assignments, he would not have believed that person. What was happening to him?

Shaking his head, he clipped the telephone to the waistband of his pants and returned to the table where Perry Reilly turned the conversation to more general talk of weather and summer activities. Andres listened but said very little. His mind returned again and again to the unexpected telephone call from Hatteras Island.

He should have been experiencing a sense of elation after hearing the wonderful news from his editor. The assignment he had always wanted was now his. He was going to the West Bank as soon as his doctors signed his medical releases, so why did he not feel the joy he imagined he would have at such a time in his life?

As he tried to focus on Perry Reilly's words, he struggled with a mixture of disorganized thoughts and emotions. He had Andy to consider now. When he left for the Middle East this time, he would be leaving behind his daughter. In addition to the little curly haired girl, he would also be leaving her exuberant blue-eyed brother.

He sighed as he acknowledged that he would have to figure out a way to tell the small boy about his imminent departure. Would the youngster understand that he just could not simply call and reach Andres anytime to tell him about Western movies airing on television? Communication in that part of the world was often unpredictable and unreliable. Tanner would not be able to press the speed-dial button and speak with him the instant he wanted to talk.

He closed his eyes for a moment, and Eve's pretty,

smiling face flashed through his mind. With sparkling green eyes, a trail of freckles across the bridge of her button nose, and thick, wavy strands of auburn hair, the image created a breathtaking picture of femininity and motherhood, of natural beauty and patient nurturing.

A sinking feeling in the pit of his stomach suddenly made him nauseous. The idea of informing Eve of his new assignment in Israel seemed almost too daunting to consider. How would he tell her? He knew it would not be an easy or enjoyable task.

Andres watched his editor push back his chair. The silver haired man smiled at him.

"I'm afraid I have another appointment right now. Shall we meet later at my office and work out some specifics of your transfer to Palestine? After four this afternoon, my schedule is fairly blank, and I'd like to take some time to give you a bit of background about what Walton has been doing in Tel-Aviv."

Four o'clock? Andres glanced at his watch. If he stayed to meet with Perry Reilly, he would not get back to Buxton until nearly midnight. There would be no chance of seeing Andy before she went to bed or to watch any part of a Western movie with Tanner.

When he listened to her voice on the telephone, Eve had sounded tired. She said that she and the children had done yard work all morning. She probably could use a little break. He remembered how refreshed and relaxed she had appeared after returning from the bubble bath she had taken at the Wetmores the day they had raked and spread mulch in the flowerbeds.

She did not get much time alone. Caring for two young, energetic children left little personal time for herself. In addition to caring for Tanner and Andy, she had spent the entire past week waiting on him and seeing to it that he rested and recovered from his leg injury. Now he acknowledged the powerful desire he had to return to Hatteras Island as soon as possible and to offer to help her if he could.

Realizing that his editor was waiting for an answer, Andres shook his head. "I'm sorry, Perry, but I really don't have the time today. There are some things I need to take care of back in Buxton first. Let's set up a meeting for early next week, okay?"

"Well, yes." The older man studied him for a moment. "You aren't having second thoughts, are you, my boy?"

"Of course not. I have to work out a few details in my personal life before I start focusing on a new assignment. I promise that I will get everything settled over the weekend and be prepared to sit down with you early Monday morning to discuss the details of going to the West Bank."

"Fine, then." Perry Reilly rose to his feet. "Give me a call when you get back to Washington."

Chapter Nine

"I'm sorry I'm so late, Eve. I planned to arrive much earlier, but the traffic all the way from Richmond was uncooperative." Andres held Tanner in his arms and stepped past Eve into the galley kitchen. Dropping a large brown envelope, he hugged the child, who was in full cowboy attire. "It's good to see you, *mi charro.*"

"The movie's almost over, but there's another one coming on right after it." Tanner bounced against him. "Come on, Andres. We're missing the best part."

Eve hid her irritation behind a forced smile. Eleven o'clock. The man had no understanding of the importance of a child's bedtime.

"No more movies, Tanner. This one is it." She spoke to her son as she met the dark brown eyes of the tall man standing near her. His tanned face looked tired and drawn, but the curve of his lips into a smile melted a little of her annoyance. "When it's done, you're going to bed."

"We'd better go watch the ending then." He set the little boy on his feet and took his hand. "Lead the way, partner."

Despite her initial anger at Andres' total disregard for her young son's bedtime routine, she could not help but appreciate the scene before her. Tanner was obviously overjoyed to be sitting next to the handsome, broad-shouldered man who listened with quiet attentiveness to both the film and Tanner's comments about the plot.

She could not ignore the child's fondness for and absolute acceptance of Andres in his life. Would the little boy survive the shock of Andres' departure when the man he admired suddenly decided to leave and to return to his reckless and dangerous profession halfway around the world?

Eve tried to focus on the suede vest she was hemming. The repetitive movements of the hand-sewing task was as automatic as awareness of Andres' presence in the room seemed to take control of her senses. Even though he was sitting several feet away from her, his closeness threatened her concentration. The faint smell of his musky aftershave floated around her head. The timbre of his voice, quiet and deep, caused her heartbeat to flutter.

She could not stop the distressing thoughts rushing through her mind. Andres would be leaving, of course. She was sure of that fact. He would go, and the empty space he left would fill with sadness. The hollow would be so big and vast that she wondered if she would ever feel completely whole or happy again.

The time she had spent without Andres during the past days while he was in Washington had seemed endless, and it had not helped to have to answer her children's frequent questions about him and his next return to Hatteras Island.

When he goes, I will miss him as much as the children will, but I won't be able to show it. I'll have to be strong for them.

Andres' absence from their lives would be a loss almost as bad as a death. That realization caused her chest to constrict.

She exhaled a breath she had been holding as a commercial began. She continued to sew while Tanner talked.

"My grandpa called today. He says he and Grandma are coming next week."

"Does that mean you have a new little cousin?"

Looking up from the suede vest, Eve saw her son nod. "A girl named Elizabeth Eve, after Mom, except Mom's Eve Elizabeth. We're going to have a family reunion here next month, and my new cousin Elizabeth will get to meet everybody, just like you will."

"A Bennett family reunion. That sounds really fun, *mi charro*, but I'm not sure I'll still be here then."

Tightness twisted in Eve's stomach as she watched disappointment mix with surprise on the little boy's face. With reluctance, she looked down at her sewing again.

"Why not? Don't you want to meet everybody?"

"Of course I do, but I might have to go back to work. The doctors say my leg is getting better, thanks to the wonderful job you and your mom did taking care of me last week."

"We shouldn't have done such a good job."

"Tanner. That wasn't very nice."

"I'm sorry, but I don't want Andres to go. I want him to stay and be Andy's dad." The little boy's shoulders drooped. "I wish he could be my dad too."

At that point, the commercial break ended, and the child returned his attention to the final scene of the Western. Eve watched Tanner lean against Andres' arm.

A heavy, numbing sensation gripped her when she saw the man sitting beside her son slip a tanned, muscular arm sprinkled with dark whorls of hair around the little boy's shoulders. *I wish he could be your dad too, Tanner.*

As the movie concluded and an announcement of the next film's title and brief summary came over the air, Tanner looked over at her with pleading in his bright, blue eyes. "Just one more, Mom? I'm not tired at all."

She slid the sharp end of the needle into the suede fabric and then set the vest on the stand next to her chair. "It's time to change into your pajamas. You need to get some sleep."

"Aw, Mom—"

"It's hours past your bedtime, Tanner. As it is, you'll probably be too tired for the neighborhood barbecue tomorrow."

Tanner leaned closer to Andres. "I don't want to go to a dumb old party. I want to stay home with Andres. We can spend the day fishing."

Andres smiled down at the little boy. "Are you talking about the party at the Hasley family's house? I received an invitation for it on my voice mail. I thought it sounded fun. I hear that there'll be games and swimming and a picnic. Are you sure you don't want to go, *mi charro*?"

"Really? You're going to the party?"

"I thought I would, but only if my fishing buddy was willing to give up the afternoon to go too. I wouldn't want to go without him. What do you say? Should you and I go and help your mother watch your sister?"

"Can we, I mean, may we go fishing on Sunday then?"

Andres glanced over at Eve. "As long as your mother doesn't have other plans for you."

Eve forced a smile. "If fishing off the dock in the backyard is okay. I thought we'd stay home and just relax on Sunday. Maybe we'll fill up the little pool so you and Andy can splash around in the water for a while."

"Will you hook up the sprinkler that twists and turns? Andres and I can run through it and chase each other."

"No chasing. Andres has to rest his leg."

Grinning, Andres tapped the brim of Tanner's hat. "Then it's a plan? We go to the barbecue tomorrow? Then fish and *walk* through the sprinkler on Sunday?"

Her son nodded as he mirrored the older male's grin. "That sounds good, partner."

Eve reached for the remote control and pressed the power button to turn off the television. "Now go get into your pajamas."

"Will you tuck me in, Andres?"

Lifting his eyebrows, he glanced back at Eve. When she nodded, he turned to her son. "I'll give you three minutes. Will you be ready by then, *mi charro*?"

The child slid off the sofa. "I'll be done in two."

"Be very quiet, Tanner. Remember that Andy's sleeping."

Andres rose to his feet as the little boy nodded and hurried down the hallway to his bedroom. "Do you mind if I look in on her?"

"No, of course not." Eve forced another smile. "She's been kicking off her blanket and sheet, but I don't want her to be cold with the air-conditioning running. Would you check to see if she needs covering up once more?"

When he returned to the living room a few minutes later, he came by way of the kitchen. Surprised, she looked up from her sewing to see him set on the low table in front of the sofa the large brown envelope he had been carrying when he arrived.

"Did Tanner settle down for you?"

His chuckle was low and deep. "I think he was asleep before I pulled the blanket up under his chin." He stuffed his hands in the pockets of his pants. "I'm really sorry about getting back so late, Eve. I know how important the children's bedtimes are to you and to them. Andy was sleeping but seemed restless when I checked on her."

"She was a little unsettled all day. She doesn't have any symptoms, but she might be coming down with a little cold or ear infection."

"Infection?"

The instant concern in his voice touched her, and her breath caught for a moment in her throat. "She'll be all right. She's had ear infections before. The pediatrician always prescribes an antibiotic suspension for her."

She watched him nod and reach for the bowl of popcorn on the table next to the brown envelope. He chewed a handful of popped kernels and swallowed before he spoke again.

"Have things been quiet around here?"

"Yes, very. Albert Clement hasn't shown up at all, at least, that I've noticed."

He chewed another mouthful of popcorn and then shook his head. "He won't be doing any more surveillance of you and the children."

She stopped hemming in mid-stitch. "How can you be so sure?"

"While I was in the Washington area, I decided to pay a visit to his Manassas office."

She leaned forward in her chair. "And he told you why he's been watching us and taking our pictures? Just like that?"

"Well, not exactly. First, I had to use a little friendly persuasion."

"That sounds rather ominous, Andres. What did you do?"

A sheepish grin pulled at the corners of his handsome mouth, and despite her agitation, her heart skipped a beat. She caught her lower lip between her teeth.

"Nothing dangerous, just some of my own investigating. I hired a private detective to do surveillance on Albert Clement."

"You had one private investigator follow another private investigator?"

He lifted his brows above deep brown eyes. "Good idea, huh?"

"It sounds kind of risky to me."

He tipped his head to one side, and the rebel strand of hair fell across his tanned forehead. "Maybe to someone who doesn't like taking risks now and then. To me, it just seemed like the next logical step."

Eve sighed and folded the edge of her shirt collar with her fingers. "So, what did you find out?"

"I discovered the identity of Albert Clement's client." Leaning toward her, he set the envelope on her lap and smiled at her. "It's all in there."

As she stared at the plain brown envelope and then looked back at him, he rose to his feet and stretched his neck from side to side. "Do you mind if I get something cold to drink?"

With trembling fingers, she turned the envelope over in her lap. "No, help yourself." She unfastened the metal clasp securing the brown flap and then glanced at him again. "You haven't had dinner, have you? I should have offered to prepare you something."

He waved a tanned hand as she started to rise. "I had a big lunch. The popcorn was fine. I just need a glass of juice." He pointed to the envelope in her hands. "Go ahead and read that report. I think it may surprise you. It definitely clears up quite a few questions we've both had regarding Mr. Clement and his recent activities here on Hatteras Island."

Minutes later, Eve was still reeling from the shock of the contents of the envelope Andres had given her when he returned to the living room with a glass of orange juice. She replaced the report and fastened the clasp with trembling hands.

"Albert Clement was investigating *me*?"

Her voice was a whisper as she asked the question that was more rhetorical in nature than one requiring any response from Andres. She held out the envelope to him.

He shook his head. "The report is yours. It is the original so you may destroy it, if you want."

She tossed the packet on the table in front of the sofa as though the idea of holding it any longer was repulsive "I can't believe someone has been questioning my ability to take care of Andy."

"No one is doubting your competence as a parent."

She stared at him. "Yes, yes, they are. That's exactly what's happening."

He squatted next to her chair and folded her trembling hands in his. "Eve, no. This whole ordeal has nothing at all to do with whether or not you are a good mother. It actually involves simple greed."

"Greed?"

"After I talked with my own investigator and then questioned Clement, I visited Cheryl's cousin, Paula, and her conniving husband, Richard. Following a few minutes of shock because they did not think I was alive, they hurried to try to explain their inexcusable behavior and admitted they had hired Clement to find evidence that you were a less than adequate choice as a permanent legal guardian for Andy."

"But why would they do such a thing? I don't understand. Cheryl's cousin and her husband?"

"Their goal was to get their hands on Andy's trust fund."

She blinked, trying to understand his words. "Andy's what?"

"Somehow Paula and Richard learned about the trust fund Cheryl had set up for Andy when she was born."

"I don't know what you're talking about."

"You didn't know that Cheryl established a million-dollar account for Andy?"

Eve felt her eyes widen. "How much?"

Andres held her gaze. "You didn't know, did you? I guess my ex-wife kept important secrets from both of us."

"I know there's a medical account, in case something serious ever happens to Andy, but I've never used it. My health insurance from work has good coverage and has always paid for doctor's bills and prescriptions."

She inhaled a deep breath as Andres continued to hold her hands. "And Cheryl said she set up a college fund for Andy, but she never mentioned a trust fund. A million dollars?"

"Cheryl's parents were very wealthy, and Cheryl inherited the Roberts family money when they died. She, herself, made an excellent living as a model, so establishing such a large trust fund would not have put a burden on her financial situation."

The amount was too great to comprehend. Eve caught her lower lip between her teeth. "So what happens now? Is Cheryl's cousin really going to try to get custody?"

He shook his head. "She can't. She has no grounds. You read the report. Clement found no proof at all to suggest you are less than a perfect mother. Anyway, she has no legal stand."

Smiling, he reached up with one hand and caressed her trembling chin with his fingertips. "Since I am named on Andy's birth certificate as her father, I am the one with the legal right to choose a guardian for her in my absence. I made it clear to Paula and Richard that I'm giving that responsibility to you."

His touch caused a tingling sensation along her jaw-line. She swallowed as she breathed in a faint scent of his familiar musky aftershave. Her stomach quivered.

"I'm glad Albert Clement won't be bothering us any-more." A series of confusing thoughts raced through her mind as she stared into his warm brown eyes. "But this is all very unnerving."

He nodded as he moved back to the couch and met her gaze. "I know, Eve."

Clearing her dry throat, she squeezed her hands in her lap. She had to ask the question that was still on her mind. "Do you know when you will be returning to work?"

He shrugged. "A couple of weeks, maybe three. As soon as my doctors give their okay."

"And you have no idea how long you'll be gone?"

"No, I never really know for certain. At least six months."

Six months? "Andy will have changed so much in that time."

"Maybe you can take some photographs and e-mail them to me."

Eve swallowed. "Pictures can't possibly represent a child's development, Andres. Soon Andy will be old enough to understand that you're her father. Aren't you concerned that she'll question why you choose a job of danger and intrigue in countries halfway around the world instead of family dinners and bedtime stories?"

He smiled, and she tried to push her growing dread to the back of her mind. "That's why I'm so grateful she has you, Eve. You can provide my daughter with all of the stability and safety and love she needs while I'm away from her."

"And you don't think that, as her father, you should be a little more involved in her life?"

"She adores you. Andy believes you are her mother. I doubt that she will miss me that much."

Eve reached for Tanner's vest on the table next to her chair. "I think you're wrong, Andres. Children can become quite attached to adults in a short time. Look at Tanner. He's already dreaming of having a father just like you. He has such faith. He waited and waited tonight for you to come. He was so sure you would."

"I know, Eve, and I'm sorry I didn't make it here sooner. I planned to be here before his bedtime."

She shook her head. "One late night won't hurt him. It's the weeks and months of not knowing where you are or when you'll be coming home that concerns me. I worry about the disappointment and sadness Andy and Tanner will both experience when you *do* visit and then have to leave again."

Several moments of silence settled in the air as Eve began her sewing in earnest. She knew if she said another word, she would more than likely be unable to stop angry tears from spilling, and she was not about to cry in front of Andres Nunez. As she made careful stitches in the thick suede fabric, she felt him watching her.

"Is that another outfit for Tanner?"

The sound of his quiet voice sent her heart racing. She tried to steady her own voice with long, deep breaths before she answered him.

"He's been watching a public broadcasting channel that's airing a series on New Mexico."

"Really?"

"Last night, he made me rush in to see what kinds of outfits the ranchers were wearing on the show. He insisted I make him a vest and shirt just like they had."

"You made a vest simply by looking at one on television?"

She continued to hem the bottom of the garment in her lap. "It's not really that hard."

She sensed him leaning toward her although she refused to pull her eyes from her work. Another lump formed in her throat.

"I think you often fail to give yourself enough credit, Eve Bennett. You have many wonderful talents."

Silence fell between them again. The house was still, and the ticking of the clock on the living room wall was the only sound Eve heard for a few moments.

"My grandmother used to sew like that. I wish you could have met her. I think the two of you would have gotten along quite well."

"You said you still have relatives in New Mexico?"

"Yes, my father's brother and his wife and their children live there. We own my grandfather's ranch together, and my uncle and his one of his sons run it in my absence."

"Do you think you'll ever go back?"

"To visit, yes. To live? I'm not sure. My life is so different now."

"Your family must miss you."

"Perhaps. We don't keep in regular contact, but at Christmastime, I usually get cards with notes reminding me to go to see them. Someday, I'll take Tanner and Andy and you to New Mexico to visit the Nunez ranch and meet my family."

"That's a nice idea." She took a moment to look at him before returning to her work. "But you shouldn't make promises you can't keep."

Again, a heavy silence hung between them. She heard him shift his weight on the sofa.

When he spoke, his voice was low, and his words precise. "It is a promise I have every intention of keeping, Eve."

"All well-meaning intentions are immaterial if a car bomb kills you."

The words caught in her throat before coming out as barely a whisper. She raised tentative eyes to meet his. "How would I explain that to your daughter or to my son?"

Distracted by her distress, she was not concentrating on her sewing when she shoved the needle into her thumb. As the sharp point penetrated her skin, she uttered an exclamation of surprise, and tears filled her eyes before she could stop them.

In an instant, Andres was squatting before her. "What is it? What's wrong?"

"Oh, nothing." She shook her head. Pulling a tissue from the box on the stand near her chair, she wrapped it around her injured thumb. "I just pricked my finger."

"Let me see."

Her heart fluttered as the sound of his soft urging reached her ears. When his hand brushed her wrist, tears spilled down her cheeks.

"No, no. I'm okay."

He rubbed her arm with his fingertips. "You don't sound okay."

With an odd sense of foreboding and fascination, she raised her eyes to meet his. She did not want to be so close to him. She did not want to feel his touch, to breath in his musky masculine scent, or to experience the effects of his dynamic personality.

On the other hand, she could not ignore the pull he had on her. Through her tears, she studied his face for a moment, taking in details that she had seen many times before then but that she seemed to be noticing for the first time. The tanned planes and angles of his face and his high cheekbones revealed his Spanish ancestry. His appealing mouth reminded her of warm smiles and teasing grins, and his incredible, deep brown eyes sparkled with a mixture of emotions.

Before she realized what he was doing, he had taken the vest from her lap and set it on the nearby stand. Holding her gaze, he grasped her elbows with the kind of extraordinary gentleness she had observed him using with Andy and Tanner and drew her to her feet.

The air was alive with his nearness as she tried to steady her legs. Shifting toward him, she trembled with restless anticipation. For once, she simply wanted to feel the strength of his arms around her and to experience the wonder and delight of his nearness.

His gaze held hers with the powerful magnetism he possessed. She watched as he leaned toward her. His mouth was so close to hers, and yet, she did not stop him.

Somewhere in her mind, she realized that he was about to kiss her. She acknowledged that fact and still she wanted him to do just that, to press his lips to hers and give her the pleasure she knew awaited them, if only she permitted it to happen.

"Eve."

She heard him whisper her name and felt his breath against her cheek. Her heart leaped, and the room seemed to fill with his presence.

A strange combination of expectancy and trust took control of her, and she moved to make smaller the remaining space between them. His hands cupped her shoulders.

She felt his breath on her face again, and then he lowered his head. Even though she welcomed it, the actual touch of his lips on hers made her dizzy. Her legs were unsteady as she shivered.

He slipped his arms around her waist as his mouth used gentle caresses to explore her lips. With slow, lingering kisses, he seemed to be coaxing her to respond.

She shuddered and lifted her arms to his neck. With her hands, she smoothed the taut cords there before combing her fingers through the soft strands of his thick, short hair.

She kissed him with the same kind of slow, lingering caresses that he had used to delight her. Never in her life had she experienced such a unique and heightened combination of tenderness and pleasure. Never had kissing been so enjoyable to her.

As her joy soared, she knew that she should stop. No good could come from participating in such an intimate activity with Andres Nunez, regardless of how wonderful his kisses proved to be.

Closing her eyes, she took a step back away from him. She inhaled deep, steady breaths and willed her heartbeat to resume a regular rhythm.

When she looked up at him again, his eyes were also closed. As he slid his hands down to rest on her hips, he heaved a slow, labored sigh.

She watched his eyes flutter open as dark lashes edged his look of obvious astonishment from the experience they had just shared. She wondered if he had enjoyed it as much as she had.

When he spoke, his hoarse words forced her back to reality and common sense. "I'm sorry, Eve. I probably shouldn't have done that."

Her hands reached up to pull at the collar of her blouse as regret replaced the former feelings of pleasure that, in an instant, had washed away with his words. Her lips still throbbed with remembrance of his tender caresses, and she swallowed.

"No, that probably wasn't a good idea."

He set his forehead against hers as she listened to his rapid breathing return to normal. She knew she had to put space between them, to move away from him before the desire to kiss him again overwhelmed her.

She cleared her throat. "Let me fix you some dinner."

For a moment, he stood very still, as though he were trying to process her words. Then he moved his hands to her shoulders and met her gaze with his dark eyes.

A chuckle rumbled in his throat, and he shook his head. "No, I don't think I'm hungry right now."

Eve studied the emotion in the depths of his deep brown eyes. She was sure that their kissing had affected him with as much power as it had her, but she knew she needed to be sensible.

She swallowed again, and with firm resolve, she took two more small steps away from him. "I'll make you a sandwich."

She hoped she did not appear as nervous and awkward as she felt when she hurried away from him into the kitchen. Selecting cold cuts, sliced cheese, fresh vegetables, and a jar of mayonnaise from the refrigerator, she inhaled slow, deep breaths once again.

Her hands were shaking as she took a plate from the cupboard and set two slices of wheat bread on it. Hearing him enter through the dining room area, she concentrated on spreading mayonnaise on each piece and avoiding his probing gaze.

Out of the corner of her eyes, she saw him lean against a nearby counter. Her stomach somersaulted, and despite the trembling of her fingers, she forced them to unwrap a package covered with clear plastic and to peel slices of provolone cheese from the pile. She could feel his eyes watching every movement.

"I don't need a sandwich.'

"You said you didn't have dinner."

"I didn't, but you don't have to wait on me."

"I'm not waiting on you. You're a guest."

She heard him sigh. "I'd like to think I'm more than a guest. We have an unusual relationship, but I'm certainly more than your guest, I hope."

Unusual? She added slices of roast beef to one piece of bread and then washed some lettuce leaves in the sink.

"Yes, I guess it is unusual."

"You're the mother of my daughter, Eve. That gives us a unique connection."

Pulling a paper towel from the roll, she patted the romaine leaves dry. With careful movements, she set the lettuce on top of the meat.

"I'm not sure I can explain what happened just now in the living room." When he reached out and touched her arm, she jumped. "Please, stop fussing with that sandwich and look at me."

Unable to control the trembling of her hands, she turned toward him and raised reluctant eyes to meet his. On his tanned face, she saw obvious apprehension and concern. *For me? For this whole situation?*

"I'm sorry I upset you. I started out trying to offer you some comfort. You had hurt your finger. You were shocked about the report regarding Albert Clement's investigation and about my new assignment. I just wanted to hold you and to try to cheer you up a little."

"Yes, of course. I understand. It's okay, Andres." She forced a smile.

"It's not okay. You're more upset than ever. Look at you. You're shaking all over."

She nodded. "You've given me a lot to think about." In addition to the investigation and his new assignment, she worried about her intense reaction to his amazing kisses. They would definitely be difficult to get out of her mind.

"I know." He took her hands and gave them a gentle squeeze. "How can I convince you that I won't abandon my daughter? I might not know as much about parenthood as you do, but Andy is very important to me. I've grown close to her. I plan to remain in her life."

"I know you plan to . . ." She caught her bottom lip between her teeth as her voice trailed off into the silence.

His brown eyes studied her for a moment before clasping with one hand the medal hanging around his neck. "I'm not going to die, Eve."

She felt her eyes widen. "How can you say that? You're going right back to that dangerous job. I don't profess to understand the intricacies of your work, but I read the newspapers and watch the news. That whole Middle East region is politically unstable. There are militant groups committing unpredictable and vicious acts of terrorism almost every day."

She inhaled another deep breath. "That's where you're going, right? Back to Iraq?"

She saw a shadow cross his face. *Oh, no. What now?*

He rubbed her knuckles with the pads of his thumbs. "To the Middle East, yes, but I won't be going back to Baghdad. I'm being reassigned to the West Bank in Palestine."

"Where? Israel? You're going to Israel? Aren't the Palestinians and the Israelis always fighting each other? Oh, Andres."

"Eve." He drew her into his arms. "I'm going to be all right. Everything will be all right."

Feeling defeated, she rested her head against his muscular shoulder but took little comfort in his embrace. She shook against his solid chest.

"You can't know that," she finally said. "You can't guarantee that your decision to go to Israel won't result in Andy becoming fatherless once again."

He rubbed his hands up and down her back. "Try not

to be so pessimistic. This is an incredible assignment. It's the dream of a lifetime for me. Please share my happiness."

Forcing a smile, she turned toward the cupboard. "Your sandwich is all ready. Would you like some chips to go with it?"

Chapter Ten

Eve was not looking forward to spending the day with curious yet well-meaning friends who were bound to ask her questions about the man who was accompanying her family to the neighborhood picnic at the Hasley residence. Andres Nunez's presence was having an overpowering effect on her typically calm and organized summer. *And what about his kisses?*

Arriving at Rob and Lisa Hasley's house at the far end of the quiet street, Eve helped Andres unload the car and then greeted her friends and neighbors with forced smiles and feigned cheerfulness. She introduced Andres and tried to ignore the puzzled expressions on their faces and avoid any direct inquiries about the handsome man with her. She noted that, while she attempted to evade certain questions as everyone sat down at lawn tables to eat, Andres and Tanner seemed to welcome and enjoy the attention and numerous comments of the less tactful party guests.

"Andres is Andy's dad. He's living in the house right next door to ours. You know, the Wetmore place, but he spends most of his time at our house with us."

She allowed her gaze to wander out to the point where the waters of the canal inlet met Pamlico Sound. A strong wind created a few white-capped ripples. She jumped when she felt Andres' warm hand touch hers.

"I'm impressed by the beauty of the island. Eve has been kind enough to show me some of its enchanting features."

"Andres took me horseback riding in Buxton Woods. He has a ranch with lots of horses in New Mexico, and we're going to go visit it someday."

The shrill sound of a whistle pierced the air, and Rob Hasley began to speak into a cordless microphone in his hand. Eve welcomed the interruption.

"It's time for the father-daughter and father-son competitions over near the boat launch. Anyone who wants to participate should head over to the left side of the lawn where my daughter Jaime has already started to set things up."

"Hey, Andres, do you think we could try some of the competitions?"

"You can't," one of the children seated across from

Tanner said. "Mr. Hasley said the games were for fathers and sons. That man's not your dad."

Eve watched her son square his shoulders, but then she had to turn her attention to Andy who was squirming beside her as the little girl reached for her cup of juice. Tanner's next words did not surprise Eve.

"He's my sister's dad, and if I had a dad, I'd want him to be just like Andres. He's the greatest!"

Eve glanced up as her son patted Andres on the arm. "Do we have to miss out on the games just because you're not my father yet?"

Yet? Eve did not miss the surprised looks and more raised eyebrows of the people sitting near them.

Tanner grinned. "Someday you'll be my dad. I just know it, and we'll be a real family, you and Mom and Andy and me."

A smile flashed across Andres' face as he wiped his hands with a paper napkin. "Let's go see what Jaime says. I'm sure she'll bend the rules a bit and let us try out those competitions. Don't you think so?"

Tanner's blue eyes sparkled. "Is it okay, Mom?"

Eve wondered what people would think about Andres and her son competing as partners, but the plea in Tanner's expression was difficult to resist. She nodded. "Have fun, but be careful. Remember that Andres' leg is still healing."

She saw the eyes of many people following the tall, tanned man and little blond boy as they held hands and hurried toward the competition area on the edge of the water. She could not help wondering what thoughts were running through the minds of her neighbors and friends.

Does it matter what people think? Tanner is happy.

Eve sighed as she wiped Andy's hands with a wet washcloth, set the little girl in the stroller, and secured the safety belt. Looking toward the group of adults and children preparing to begin the lively games, she noticed that despite the seriousness of his injury, Andres had already abandoned his cane. With intention or not, he had left the symbol of his temporary handicap leaning against the rough trunk of the longleaf pine shading one end of the Hasley family's lawn.

After discarding used paper plates and utensils and cups in a nearby trash container, Eve pushed Andy's stroller over the yard to a spot where she could see the ensuing contests among teams who were being cheered on and encouraged by enthusiastic spectators. With a cordless microphone, Jaime Hasley shouted directions and provided verbal descriptions of the teams' status.

Andy squealed and clapped her hands as she appeared to watch the excitement and activity from her seat in the stroller. She waved to Andres and Tanner and called out their names several times throughout the games before Rob and Jaime announced the winners and awarded ribbons and prizes.

"Can you believe it, Mom?"

"Andres and I were such a great team. A red ribbon for

the water balloon toss and another for the beach ball basketball battle. We got second place out of fifteen teams."

Tanner waved the large satin ribbons in the air. "And first place for the kite competition! I didn't think we could do it. Make a kite in ten minutes and then fly it higher than anybody? But Andres kept saying we could. He believed in us, so I did too."

With mixed feelings, Eve leaned down and hugged her son as she met Andres' dark eyes above Tanner's khaki fishing cap. She wanted to share in the little boy's joy, but at the same time, she worried about the impact Andres' leaving would have on Tanner, as well as Andy. Despite her desire to be objective about the situation, she had difficulty ignoring her own unsettled emotions.

How could I let my feelings get so involved? Why did I allow myself to fall in love with Andres Nunez?

"Pick me up, Noo-noo."

"Hey, Tanner. You and Mr. Nunez were amazing." Jaime Hasley approached Eve and her family as Andres leaned down to lift Andy from her stroller.

A broad smile covered the teenager's face. "You worked together as though you've been teaming up for competitions like these for a long time."

Tanner beamed. "Andres and I make a good pair, don't we?"

Jaime tapped the brim of the little boy's cap and then reached out to smooth Andy's curls as the child bounced against her father's chest. "You certainly do."

She narrowed her eyes at Tanner. "Are you sure you

didn't find out about the games I chose for this picnic and start practicing with Mr. Nunez so you'd be ready for today?"

The little boy shook his head. "No, Jaime. Really. We didn't know anything about them."

Rob Hasley approached them. He carried several double-bladed paddles.

"Hey, Dad, are things set up for the adult competitions?"

"We're just getting ready now. Eve, you and Andres are going to join in the fun, aren't you?"

"Oh, I can't, Rob. The kids—"

"I'll watch Tanner and Andy." Jaime smiled at Eve. "I don't get to spend very much time with them anymore."

"Then it's settled? You and Andres will be partners?" Rob held out a paddle to her. "We thought the two of you would want be together since we understand that congratulations are in order."

"Congratulations?" Without knowing why, Eve raised her gaze to meet Andres' dark brown eyes.

"On your engagement. Several people have mentioned your upcoming wedding plans."

"Wedding? Hey, Mom, why didn't you tell me? That's great!" Tanner hopped up and down as he waved his ribbons in the hot summer air. "Andres is going to be my dad. I'm going to get my wish!"

Stunned, Eve waited for a moment, expecting that Andres would jump into the conversation with a steadfast denial, but instead, he simply shrugged his broad shoulders. With growing dismay, she watched a smile spread across his face.

"Well, thank you, Rob." He shifted Andy from one arm to the other. "Eve and I haven't made any specific plans yet, but a wedding in the future is a definite possibility."

He winked at Eve and then handed his daughter to Jaime. "Be good, *mi niñita* Rosita. You and Tanner are going to stay with Jaime while your mother and I show off our talents in the water sports events."

He kissed the top of Andy's head and reached out to shake Tanner's hand. "Wish us luck, *mi charro*. I've never used one of these double-bladed paddles."

Eve was shaking her head in complete shock. Her head spun with thoughts that swirled in every direction.

"Here, Mom, you need something to keep the sun off your head. Take my fishing cap."

As she accepted the hat from her son, Rob thrust a kayak paddle into her hand. She felt Andres slip an arm around her waist and steer her toward the water's edge where several vessels of various colors waited, lined up along the sand. Her head ached. The rocking of the bows of the boats caused by the rhythmic movement of the gentle waves made her stomach tumble.

"Choose any two-seater kayak." Rob gestured toward the array of watercraft. "There are several canoes, but I think you'll prefer a kayak, Eve."

Her neighbor patted Andres on the back. "You'd better let Eve sit at the stern. She'll be able to steer from there and still give you some pointers on how to paddle."

Before she had a chance to verbalize her objections, Andres had bent his long legs and twisted into the front seat of a bright yellow kayak while Rob steadied it with his hands. She had a vague awareness of other couples around them boarding similar watercraft. Out in the sound, she saw choppy water creating white caps along the surface.

"In you go, Eve. Now, the object of this competition is to paddle out to the red buoy, circle it, and return here to the starting point before the others arrive. First place is dinner for two at the Cape Inn in town."

Andres turned and grinned back at her as she took her seat behind him. "Sounds nice. We could use a night out just for the two of us. Let's get this thing going, Eve."

The weightless sensation of sitting in the kayak on the surface of the water caused Eve's stomach to somersault as she studied Andres' back and shoulders covered with the thin cotton material of his loose shirt. She heard a whistle and then saw kayaks and canoes surrounding them and racing toward the red buoy in the distance.

A spray of warm salt water struck her face as Andres fumbled with his paddle. Water splashed all over them and pooled in the bottom of the vessel.

"Hey, we're just going in circles, aren't we?"

She forced herself to concentrate on the task of trying to keep the kayak afloat and pointed in the direction of the buoy out in Pamlico Sound. She groaned in silence as water soaked through the white canvas of her espadrilles.

"Try not to slap the water, Andres. You're hitting the surface with the flat part of your paddle. Instead, you want to *cut* the water. On only the left side of the kayak, slice the water with the edge of the blade, like a knife."

Adjusting Tanner's hat on her head, she waited while he followed her instructions. After a few tries, he was maneuvering the paddle better than she would have expected after so little time to practice.

"Now do the same on the right side."

Again, he impressed her with his apparent natural prowess in managing the double-bladed paddle. Was there anything Andres Nunez could not do or, at least, was not willing to attempt?

"Okay, good. Now you need to put both sides together, still slicing and not slapping. Try to establish a comfortable speed at which you can maintain a continual motion with the paddle. Keep your back straight and roll your shoulders as you move your arms."

"Aye, aye, captain."

When he twisted around and grinned at her, the kayak rocked from side to side with precarious movements that sent Eve's stomach into nauseous spasms once again. The breeze had become strong and gusty as they left the protection of the canal and approached the water of the open sound. They were within a few hundred feet of the red buoy.

Wind whipped around Eve's head and caught the

brim of Tanner's cap. Lunging to the right, she realized too late that Andres was, at the same time, making an attempt to retrieve the fishing hat, as well. The right side of the kayak dipped into the water and then overturned, sending both of them into the sound.

When she realized that the kayak was capsizing, she had inhaled a quick breath at the last minute and plunged into the cool depths. Her shorts and tank top made swimming almost effortless, and after kicking off her espadrilles, she was able to skim along the sandy bottom for several long strokes.

"Eve! Eve!"

From somewhere far away, she heard someone call her name. For a moment, she allowed the water all around her to soothe her agitated nerves, but then she remembered Andres' injured leg.

"Eve!"

With strong, precise strokes, she swam toward the surface. Filling her lungs with air, she treaded water with her feet as she tried to wipe her eyes dry with her hands.

"Eve, there you are! I couldn't find you."

Andres was swimming toward her with strong, even strokes. The evidence of his relief shone in his dark, concerned eyes. With the fingers of one hand, he reached out and brushed a strand of wet hair from her forehead.

"You had me worried, *mi querida*. I thought I'd lost you."

She stopped treading water as the raw emotion of his voice filled her ears. She felt his hands encircle her waist, holding her with firm support so her head stayed above the surface of the water.

"Eve, are you all right?"

She swallowed and again began to move her feet in a rhythmic motion. "Yes, yes, I'm fine."

Looking toward the nearest shore, she saw a small sand beach marking a place several hundred yards from where they had capsized the kayak. She pointed. "We'd better swim toward land."

"Can you make it? Do you need help?"

She shook her head, still very much aware of his hands at her waist. "No, do you? How's your leg?"

"It's starting to cramp up, but I can make it to that little beach." He removed one hand from beneath the surface of the water and held up her son's water-drenched fishing hat.

"I saved Tanner's cap, by the way."

She could not help but smile. "Now you're my hero too. I'll follow you, in case your leg gives you trouble."

"No, I want to keep my eye on you."

Her leg muscles were beginning to tire. "Okay, then. We'll swim together, side by side."

Although his strokes were stronger, Eve found that she could match his speed most of the distance. When she did lag behind him a few times, she noticed that he adjusted his rate of movement until she was able to catch up to him. She pulled herself onto the empty beach and flopped down on the warm sand as he followed. They were almost a mile away from the nearest house.

Trying to regulate her breathing, she inhaled great gulps of air as she squeezed water from her hair. Andres lowered himself down beside her, and for a few moments, they did not speak.

Leaning back on her elbows, she closed her eyes and lifted her face to the bright afternoon sun. She felt the heat begin to dry her skin at once.

Andres' fingertips traced her cheekbone and jawline. The gentle caresses sent pulses of warmth unrelated to the summer sun along her neck, shoulders, and arms.

"You're sure you're okay, *mi querida?*"

"Mm." She nodded as she allowed herself to enjoy the feathery softness of his touch. "I'm fine. Just a little wet. What does *mi querida* mean?"

He rested his fingers on her chin, and she opened hesitant eyes to him. He was looking at her with a steady, intense gaze.

"It means 'my darling' or 'my dear.'" He inhaled a long, slow breath. "You scared me, Eve. My heart is still pounding. I've definitely decided to get you a Saint Isidore medal to protect you in just such situations as this."

Darling? Dear? She smiled. "There was no reason to worry. I'm a fairly competent swimmer."

She watched a shadow cross his face. "Luis was a good rider for his age, but I still lost him."

"Luis? Your brother?"

Nodding, he turned to stare out across the water. "I couldn't save him. A rattlesnake spooked our horse.

When the stallion reared up, Luis fell and struck his head. When the kayak capsized on us and we fell into the water, I couldn't find you. I was sure you had hit your head too."

He turned back to her, and his expression was bleak. "When I called your name and you didn't come to the surface, I was afraid the same thing had happened to you."

Eve reached out and squeezed his hand. "Those are the memories that have been giving you nightmares, the ones about your brother's death? Not the dangerous conditions of your job?"

He chuckled, but his expression was still grave. "My grandmother used to say that Luis's death was the reason I chose the profession I did. She said I wanted to test life and defy death. That's why she insisted I enlist the protection of the Spanish patron saint of farmers, Saint Isidore. She always thought my recklessness required a special kind of spiritual guardianship."

To test life and defy death. Those words certainly seemed to describe Andres Nunez's impulsive and, often, perilous behaviors, especially concerning his work.

Eve inhaled a deep breath. "It was an accident, Andres. You must not blame yourself for Luis's death."

"He was my little brother."

"It wasn't your fault."

"In my mind, I know that's true, but in my heart I feel responsible."

"I think your heart and your feelings often interfere with your mind."

He grinned. "Maybe they do. My feelings for you and Andy and Tanner pulled me back here to Hatteras Island last night when my mind had made the decision to stay in Washington and finalize plans for my new assignment."

Her chest tightened at the mention of his imminent departure from her life. She gazed back down the point where she could barely see the beach on the Hasley property.

"People will be wondering where we are." Although she had brought up the subject of feelings, she did not want to talk about them, especially her own.

Andres nodded. "A few of the contestants lagging behind saw us, but when they realized we were both okay, I guess they continued paddling."

"I think you'll find that most of the neighbors have a very competitive spirit."

"And when faced with the choice of being good Samaritans or winning a dinner for two, there's no contest?"

"I'm afraid not."

"Then I suppose it's safe to say that we have no chance of winning first prize?"

She wiggled her toes in the sand. "It's at least a twenty-minute walk back. I think we'll probably miss the rest of the contests. Do you mind terribly?"

"Not at all. I'm just glad that you're okay." He lifted her hand and rubbed her fingernails with the pad of his thumb. "In fact, I prefer your company to any one of your interesting neighbors, Eve."

Her breath caught in her throat at the sound of his soft words. She recalled his bewildering refusal to deny the rumors spreading around the neighbors at the picnic earlier that day.

"Why did you let Rob Hasley and the others think we were engaged to be married?"

He raised his brows above deep brown eyes. "Does it really matter what people think? We like each other, don't we? We're friends. We share a common goal."

She dug her toes into the warm sand. "What goal is that?"

"To raise Andy to adulthood, of course. To help her lead a happy, fulfilling life."

She narrowed her eyes at him. "Is that really your goal, Andres, or is yours just to show up occasionally when such a visit fits into your plans? Will Andy ever come first, or will breaking news in Palestine or Iraq or some other faraway place always be more exciting and more important than your daughter?"

The sound of an engine caused her to turn as she watched a dark sport utility vehicle approaching. When it stopped, Rob Hasley and another neighbor jumped out and hurried toward them.

"Are you all right? We saw your kayak tip over, but from shore we couldn't tell what happened."

"We're fine, Rob, but we could probably use a ride back to your house. I lost my shoes, and Andres shouldn't be walking that far on his injured leg."

She glanced at the man sitting next to her. "I'm

afraid we didn't have a chance to retrieve the kayak and paddles."

"I'll send some of the kids out to get them. We're just glad you're both okay."

Andres rose to his feet and held out a hand to Eve. "Are you sure you don't mind giving us a lift? We're still really wet and covered with sand."

Rob opened the back door behind the driver's seat. "We take this rig to the beach every weekend. It's always wet and sandy."

Eve made a feeble attempt to brush sand from her feet and clothing before sliding into the backseat. She felt Andres' gritty leg brush against hers as he slid in beside her. Her heart began to race again. If Andres Nunez were going away, she thought, he had better leave soon, or her poor heart would never last.

Just as Andres had promised, he spent most of the day Sunday fishing with Tanner on the dock behind Eve's parents' cottage. When he was not casting a line, reeling in a fish, or discussing angling techniques and types of bait with her son, he tried to entertain and console his uneasy daughter.

Andy had whined and fussed and begged to be held all day long. She did not want to eat or sleep or play.

By Sunday evening, Eve was concerned that the child was developing some kind of illness, but when she took Andy's temperature, the little girl did not have a fever. Eve read to her, took her for walks, sang her songs, and tried to make her as comfortable as possible.

When Andres announced that he would be heading back to Washington as soon as the children went to bed, Eve faced her disappointment with firm resolve. She had lived without Andres Nunez before she met him, so she could certainly manage without him again.

She stopped her pacing in front of the glass doors of the living room and dining area as Andres strode from Tanner's room at bedtime. She patted Andy's back as the child began to whimper.

"He was asleep before I turned the second page of the book."

Eve nodded. "He's exhausted. He's had an extremely busy weekend."

Andres reached out and brushed her cheek with his fingers. "You look exhausted too. Why don't you let me walk with Andy for a while so you can sit down?"

For a few moments, she enjoyed the warmth of his gentle touch. Then, with careful movements, she placed the dozing child in his arms. Eve watched the little girl snuggled against his blue polo shirt.

"I love you, Noo-noo."

Andy's voice was a hoarse whisper as one small hand reached up to grasp the sterling silver medal around his neck. "Rock me, Noo-noo."

He lowered himself into the white wooden rocking chair and settled the child on his lap. He moved back and forth in slow, smooth motions, as though he had been comforting children for years.

Eve's chest tightened. Andres was a wonderful father when he chose to be a part of his daughter's life. Both Andy and Tanner would benefit from his consistent presence, but she was not sure that any good could come from his decision to stay away from them for long periods of time.

"Do you think she's sick?"

Eve sat on the edge of the sofa. "She probably has an ear infection. I'll take her to the clinic tomorrow."

"Is there something we can give her to make her feel better right now?"

Eve saw the concern in his dark brown eyes as he continued to rock Andy. "I have a fever reducer for her if her temperature rises, but it was normal the last time I checked."

"You'll let me know what you find out at the clinic?"

"I promise to call you with any news."

"Do you think she'll sleep tonight? She hasn't napped all day."

Eve sighed. "If she's developing an ear infection, she probably won't rest very well. She usually doesn't."

"What about you?"

"Me?"

"When will you sleep if Andy keeps you up all night? You need rest too."

Her heart skipped a beat as she realized that the concern in his dark eyes was meant for her, as well as for the child in his arms. She forced a smile. "When she gets well, I'll be able to sleep again."

He pulled his gaze back to the curly head resting against his chest, and he sighed. "I wish there was a better solution than that."

He sat in silence for a few moments. "Well, I suppose I should get going. I have a long drive ahead of me. I am meeting with my editor and his staff for breakfast at seven."

"You have a lot of details to discuss about your new assignment?"

He nodded. "I'm taking over for another journalist who has requested a leave to do some other writing. The editorial staff will most likely keep me until close to lunch time."

"Would you like me to make some coffee and put it in a thermos for you?"

He smiled. "I appreciate the offer, but I'll stop and get a cup along the way. Usually my leg needs some exercise before my body needs caffeine these days."

"You'll stop if you get tired?"

"Yes, I'll pull over the minute I start to feel drowsy." He rose to his feet and placed Andy back into her arms "Before I met you, it had been a long time since anyone expressed such concern for my well-being, Eve. It's a nice feeling to know that someone is thinking about me."

Eve hugged Andy. "Just be careful. Andy loves you."

He smoothed the child's curls with his hand. "Call me as soon as you take her to the clinic, okay?"

"I will." *I love you too, Andres.*

Eve glanced at her wristwatch. *Five o'clock.*

She studied Andy's flushed cheeks and glassy eyes as the child tugged at her left ear. The little girl had been up all night.

"It won't be long now, sweetie. We'll get you some medicine to make you feel better."

"I want Noo-noo."

Eve's chest tightened at the sound of the little girl's hoarse plea. Finally, she nodded. "Let's call your daddy."

She reached for the telephone on the nearby end table. If Andres had no trouble on the road, he should have arrived at his hotel. As she pressed Andres' speed dial number, she hoped that *he*, at least, had managed to get a little sleep.

He answered on the first ring. "Yes?"

"It's Eve, Andres. Andy has a fever. She keeps asking for you."

"A fever? How high?"

"Not bad. It's holding steady at one hundred right now."

"Do you think she needs to go to the hospital?"

"The clinic will be open soon. Her temperature always rises when she gets an ear infection."

"What about you? How are you holding up?"

"I'm fine. Just tired. I think Andy wants to hear your voice."

"Well, she'll be able to hear me in person in just a few minutes. I'm pulling into your driveway now."

"What?" Her heart somersaulted as she rushed to the kitchen with Andy in her arms. When she stepped out onto the porch, she could not calm her racing pulse.

From the bottom of the stairs, Andres looked up at her and gave her a warm smile that lit up his tanned face. Taking two steps at a time, he climbed to the porch and wrapped his arms around her.

His embrace was so tight and lasted so long that Andy began to squirm in protest. "Noo-noo, let's go rock."

With a chuckle that Eve heard rumbling along the length of his chest, he released them and kissed the top of his daughter's curly head. He lifted the little girl into his arms.

"Oh, yes, *mi niñita* Rosita. We'll rock and rock as long as you want, but first I need to do something."

The rich Latin accent of his words filled Eve's ears with soft familiarity. His dark brown eyes caught her gaze, and she became aware of an instant eruption of need deep within her as she realized that he was lowering his mouth to kiss her. Tender, tentative lips brushed against hers, and a shower of warmth washed over her.

Shivering with indescribable delight, she allowed herself to lean toward him and respond to his touch. She felt his chest rise and fall as he inhaled unsteady breaths of air. She reveled at the thoughts tumbling through her mind with overpowering intensity.

With slow, reluctant movements, he raised his head and held her eyes with his. Excitement mixed with confusion as she swallowed, and her heart continued to race.

"What are you doing here, Andres?"

"I'm here to be with you."

"What about your meeting?"

He glanced down at the little girl, who appeared to be falling asleep at last. "I kept thinking about Andy. I thought about your taking her to the clinic all by yourself."

"I promised I'd call and let you know what the doctor said."

"I never doubted that you'd call, but the more I thought about it, the more I knew I should be here with you, not in Washington getting a call about Andy. I should be here when she gets sick and when Tanner and you get sick too."

"I don't usually get sick."

"Well, I should be here when your kayak capsizes, then."

"That doesn't happen very often either."

His smile faded, and his brown eyes darkened with emotion. "I want to be here when it does, Eve. I want to be with you."

"You can't be here with us and do your job too. It's impossible."

"It's not impossible." With his free hand, he laced his

fingers with hers. "I came back because I think I have a solution."

His words thrilled her for a moment and then left her desolate. She shook her head. "I don't think there is a solution. Your profession is dangerous. There's no way around that."

He squeezed her hand. "I love you, Eve."

Love me? Had she heard him say those words or had she imagined them?

She wanted him to love her. She wanted him to return the deep feelings she had for him, but she needed to think about Andy and Tanner.

"I won't put the children through such constant uncertainly in their young lives."

"I know. I know I can't be a parent just when it fits into my schedule. I can't be a *father of convenience*." He held her gaze. "I want your family to be my family. I want that more than any dream assignment in Palestine. In fact, between the two, there is really no choice."

She inhaled a deep breath as he continued to hold her hand and her gaze. "What are you saying, Andres?"

"I'm saying that I love you and Andy and Tanner more than I want this new assignment. I called my editor and woke him up to tell him that. I told him I wanted to be reassigned to the Washington office in one of the open correspondent positions there. I rescheduled our appointment to discuss that job next week, and then I turned around and headed back toward Hatteras Island."

"You're going to work in Washington?" She was still having a hard time understanding what he was telling her. "How can you be sure that you won't get bored after a few weeks and long for the excitement and danger of being an embedded journalist or undercover investigative reporter in some politically unsettled region halfway around the world?"

"I know I won't because, *mi querida*, i am in love with you." He leaned down and brushed her mouth with his lips. "I know because I don't want to live another day without you. I want to hold you in my arms and kiss you and help you raise our children. I truly do."

She felt her heartbeat quicken as she slipped her arms around his waist. "I have a small confession to make."

He raised his eyebrows. "Really?"

She rubbed her hands up and down the muscles of his back. "Andy wasn't the only one who needed to hear your voice earlier."

He grinned and reached out to touch her cheek with his fingertips. "I love you, Eve."

Epilogue

Rays of bright August sunlight glistened and reflected off the smooth surface of Pamlico Sound as Eve gazed out at the lone kayak with its rider paddling in the distance. A warm breeze blew toward the dock, and she tucked a strand of hair behind her ear.

"Look, Mommy. I caught a fish."

She smiled down at Andy as her daughter tugged on her arm. The little girl's dark curls brushed her shoulders and fell onto her pink life jacket.

"Wow, that's a keeper, Andy. I'll help you take it off the line."

Eve rubbed her lower back as she watched Tanner

use deft fingers to remove the hook from the little fish and drop it into a bucket of water. Her son had grown so much in the past year. "Dad's going to be really proud of you, Andy. Let's go show him."

"Show me what?"

Andres' quiet, Latin-accented voice reached Eve's ears, and she turned to smile at him as he strode along the dock. Her heart did a little somersault as his dark eyes caught hers.

Andy grinned and ran toward her father. "I got a fish, Daddy."

"She hooked a nice sea trout. You'll have to come see it, Dad."

"A sea trout, *mi niñita*? Did you?" Andres slipped one arm around Eve's waist as he smoothed his daughter's curly hair with the other. "Let me have a look."

"See, Daddy." Andy pointed into the plastic bucket. "Tanner says it's a keeper. Can we keep it in the bathtub?"

Tanner wrinkled his nose. "No, silly. A keeper is a fish that's big enough to eat. That sea trout will make a nice meal, won't it, Dad?"

The little girl's eyes grew wide and round. "Eat it? You want to eat my pretty fish?" Big tears rolled down her cheeks as she shook her head, causing a cascade of curls to fall across her shoulders. "No, I won't let you!"

Her brother patted her arm. "It's okay, Andy. Don't cry. We'll put your fish back in the water where it'll be happy. Let's go see how Grandpa is doing with Uncle Paul and the boys."

"Be careful." Eve watched the two children run toward the far end of the dock where her father was giving angling pointers to her brother and his three sons.

"You shouldn't be out here in this heat."

She enjoyed Andres' soft voice near her ear. Keeping her eyes on Tanner and Andy, she smiled. "I'm perfectly all right. I just put on another layer of sunscreen." She set her head against his chest. "Stop fussing over me."

He kissed her temple. "I love fussing over you, Mrs. Nunez, so you'd better just get used to it."

"Oh!"

Andres' expression turned in an instant from amusement to intense concern as she looked up at him. He tightened his hold around her waist. "What is it? What's wrong?"

Eve rubbed her palms over the thin fabric of her cotton top. "This baby is so active today. He definitely has his father's energy."

"He?"

"Or she. Maybe I'd better sit down."

Nodding, Andres led her off the dock to some wooden lawn furniture. He helped her lower herself into a chair and then leaned over to look at her, his concern still evident in his dark eyes.

"Are you sure you're okay?"

"Yes." She looked toward the end of the dock. "But I should probably go back and watch Andy and Tanner."

"Your father will watch them for a few minutes. You look tired, Eve."

He sat on the edge of the chair next to hers. "Maybe you should go inside and lie down for a while."

She smiled. "I love you too, Andres."

His expression remained serious. "I just want to make sure you and the baby are okay."

She squeezed his hand. "We're both fine. Everything is going well." She laughed. "Stop worrying."

"What's so funny?"

"I can't believe I'm the one telling *you* not to worry. I remember a time not so long ago when you were always telling me that."

He lifted her hand to his lips and kissed her fingertips. She smiled as she enjoyed the tenderness of his touch.

"I never used to think I had much to worry about. We have the final closing on the Wetmore house next week, and Tanner starts school soon. I still haven't finished painting the baby's room."

"Everything will get done, darling."

"Daddy! Come see! Tanner caught a big fish."

Eve turned and saw Andy jumping up and down on the dock as she waved her arms. "Look, Noo-noo!"

Rising to his feet and waving to his daughter, Andres looked back at Eve. "She hasn't called me that in a long time."

"She understands that you're her father. *Noo-noo* is just an affectionate nickname for the man she knows as *Daddy* now."

He nodded. "I'm so glad she and Tanner seem to have adjusted well to having me around all of the time."

"Are you kidding? They adore you. They can't imagine their lives without you, and I can't either." She smiled. "And what about you, Andres? Do you have any regrets about your new, ordinary life as a family man in Arlington, Virginia?"

A smile flashed across his tanned face. "Absolutely none. Shifting from being a father of convenience to a father—and husband—all of the time is the best career decision I have ever made."

"Daddy, come look!"

He waved again to the little girl with curly hair waiting on the dock. "I had better go and check on Tanner's big catch. Stay here and rest, *mi querida*. It is my turn to watch our children."